The Devil's Share

J.T. Southwell

Wayfinder Press

CHAPTER ONE

Harbor of Flags

The sun rose red as rust over Nassau harbor, casting a bruised light across a forest of masts. Flags of every nation hung limp in the dawn air—English crosses beside Spanish lions, French tricolors beside Dutch stripes. A republic of thieves, each ship flew whatever colors would buy it a day's peace.

The air was thick with brine and pitch, and the sour-sweet scent of rum leaking from cracked casks. Along the quay, merchants shouted in three languages, bartering over stolen sugar and powder barrels as if it were lawful trade. Somewhere beyond the bluff, a bell tolled from the little stone church, its voice swallowed by laughter spilling out of tavern doors.

Aboard *The Sable Wraith*, the noise faded into rhythm—ropes creaking, canvas slapping, boots thudding on sun-warped planks. Elias Grey moved through it all like a man following an inner compass.

His tone stayed low but carried. "Shift that cask forward, Mr. Delgado. Mind the balance."

"Aye, sir."

Nico Delgado, the ship's boatswain's mate, echoed the order down the line with practiced sharpness. Though barely past twenty, he handled men twice his age as if he'd been born to the deck. When one of the hands fumbled a lashing, Nico was there first—fingers quick, voice clipped but steady—the reflection of his teacher's restraint.

Grey checked the splice with a glance, approving silently. It wasn't perfection that mattered, but precision under pressure. He'd learned that from Locke. Everything else was noise.

Around them the harbor seethed: bare-chested dockmen rolling barrels ashore, gulls screaming overhead. On a half-sunk hulk nearby, a man with a bottle in each hand sang about freedom, forgetting the part where it cost blood. Grey ignored it. He had a ship to keep balanced—and in Nassau, that meant more than just weight and wind.

Footsteps struck the gangplank behind him—hard, uneven, drunk with their own importance.

"God's wounds, Grey!" The voice boomed across the deck. "You'll polish her till she shines brighter than a bishop's cup."

Captain Silas Redd strode aboard, boots clattering, rings flashing in the early light. His coat hung open, red silk faded to rust, the gold buttons mismatched from half a dozen stolen uniforms. He carried a bottle of something dark and mean, and the smell of it followed him like smoke.

Grey straightened but didn't salute. "She sails truer for the care, Captain."

Redd grinned, showing a silver-capped tooth. "Truer, is it? A ship's no woman, boy. She likes to be handled rough."

The crew laughed—quick, nervous laughter, like dogs testing their master's mood. Redd basked in it, eyes glittering. He turned to Nico, clapping him hard on the shoulder. "Mind him, lad. He'll scrub the devil out of you if you're not careful."

"Aye, Captain," Nico said—polite tone, wary eyes.

When Redd moved on, Grey met Nico's glance. No words passed, but the meaning did: hold steady.

Redd swaggered toward the bow, calling for the quartermaster, spitting over the side, shouting greetings to a merchant on the dock. Every motion demanded attention; every word was a small performance.
Grey watched him without expression—the way a helmsman watches storm clouds gathering far off the horizon.

By midmorning the harbor had come fully alive. Fishmongers called prices beside gunrunners. A pair of red-coated deserters loaded muskets onto a Dutch brig flying a French flag. Slaves were bartered on the same dock where a preacher held his Bible high, shouting about deliverance. Nassau was freedom made flesh—and rotting.

Grey leaned against the rail and let the sounds wash over him. Locke would have hated this place. Or perhaps he'd have understood it. "Balance," the old man used to say, "even mercy weighs something." Grey rubbed the serpent-and-anchor ring with his thumb, feeling its grooves warm against his skin. The sea breeze lifted just enough to catch his whisper. "Mercy earns consequence."

The words disappeared into the wind, swallowed by gulls and gunfire.

Behind him, Redd barked orders to cast off lines before noon. The tide, Grey knew, would run the wrong way until past two. He caught Nico's eye and spoke low. "Hold them until it turns. He'll have forgotten by then."

Nico nodded and slipped among the crew. A few murmured questions later, the men moved at Grey's pace, not Redd's. By the time the captain noticed, the sun had climbed too high for an early departure, and he was too drunk to care. The ship obeyed Elias Grey without realizing it.

A merchant came up the dock then—small, sweating, hat clutched tight in both hands. He whispered something into Redd's ear. The captain's expression sharpened; the grin that followed was too wide, too knowing.

"A Spanish brig, you say?" Redd's voice carried easily, loud enough for the men on deck to hear. "Limping north with a belly full of silver?" He laughed—hard and bright as broken glass. "Then God himself smiles on us, doesn't he?"

Grey turned, pretending not to listen, though every word landed like a weight. Spanish brigs rarely sailed alone—not with silver aboard. The convoy rumor had circled the harbor for weeks, and most captains had the sense to ignore it. Most.

Redd tossed the merchant a coin and raised his bottle in salute. "Tomorrow we dine like kings, lads! The sea's been too long without our tithe."

The crew cheered. Even those who didn't believe him cheered, because that was what Redd demanded—noise, not conviction.

Grey looked past them toward the reef, where the horizon blurred into a line of darkening cloud. Thunder muttered faintly beyond it, too distant yet to break. He traced the ring again, the way a man touches a scar to remind himself it's real.

Fortune, he thought, *always asks its due.*

CHAPTER TWO

The Captain's Table

The wind turned uneasy by noon, sliding across the harbor like a change of mood. Grey felt it in the ropes—a faint, high hum when weather begins to gather somewhere out of sight. He was checking the forward lashings when a runner called from the companionway.

"Captain wants his officers in the great cabin."

Elias wiped tar from his palms. "Aye."

Nico Delgado, the boatswain's mate, fell in behind him with a coil of line slung across one shoulder—the same excuse he always used to be where he wasn't expected.

The great cabin smelled of rum and tallow. Maps spread across the table, corners pinned by pistols and half-drained glasses. Captain Silas Redd stood behind them, sleeves rolled, expression sharp but easy.

"Gentlemen," he said, motioning them nearer. "Fortune's decided she still knows our names."

He tapped a coin against the chart where the sea between Cartagena and the Bahama Channel lay blue and wide. "A Spanish sugar brig, limping north. Holds full, crew half-sick, ballast heavy with silver. The kind of gift a man earns by being ready when she stumbles."

A few of the officers leaned in. Even the light off the harbor seemed to brighten at the word *silver*.

Redd's tone was steady, confident—the practiced voice of a man who had commanded long enough to believe in his own luck. "We come at her from windward. One broadside across the stern to cripple her, then we board and finish clean."

He looked up from the chart. "Questions?"

Elias studied the routes drawn in ink, following the coastlines with his eye. He'd heard the same rumor in the taverns—a Spanish brig carrying sugar and whispers of silver. He also knew Spain never let coin travel unguarded.

"Sir," he said carefully, "convoy out of Cartagena runs with escort—a light frigate or at least a cutter. If she's as heavy as they claim, we'll see her consort before we see her colors."

The room stayed quiet a moment. Redd's brow furrowed—not in anger but in calculation. "Noted," he said at last, voice level. "Still, no escort's been sighted from the Caicos posts, and the wind's in our favor. We'll trust to that."

Grey inclined his head. "Aye, Captain. I'll have the men ready for weather and for chase."

Redd's mouth curved faintly. "That's why you have the deck, Mr. Grey. I need a helmsman who thinks two moves ahead—even if he doesn't always like the board."

The officers chuckled; the remark carried an edge, but also recognition. Redd's tone was half-teasing, not cruel.

He poured a measure of rum into a cup and slid it down the table toward Elias. "To prudence," he said. "And to those who remind us the sea's got teeth."

Elias left the cup untouched. "Aye, sir."

Redd drank for them both, then set the glass aside. "We sail on the tide. Guns run ready, grapples checked, powder dry. The weather may wet us, but she'll wet them worse."

He flattened the map with his palm—final word. "Dismissed."

Outside, the air felt thicker, charged. Thunder rolled somewhere east of the reef.

Nico caught up beside him. "You think he's right?"

Elias shook his head once. "I think he believes he is. That's enough to get us moving."

Nico frowned. "And if there's an escort?"

"Then we keep our powder dry and our wits drier." He paused, then added quietly, "Double-wrap the cartridges, dog the lids on the boxes. If the rain hits, I don't want excuses."

"Aye, sir."

Grey glanced back toward the cabin door. He still heard Redd repeating the plan to the quartermaster—same flourish, same laughter answering him. The sound wasn't cruel, just confident. That, he thought, was the danger: confidence could sound so much like certainty.

By late afternoon the harbor swayed under a lowering sky. Men moved faster now—rope over shoulder, barrels rolling—the half-drunk cheer of morning gone. Elias oversaw the work with the same quiet patience he always carried: small corrections, a nod to Nico.

Redd came up from below, coat buttoned, sober again. The man feared in taverns became, at sea, something sharper and almost admirable—alert, alive, a predator scanning weather and water in equal measure.

"Mr. Grey," he called. "How does she sit?"

"Trimmed and ready, sir. We'll clear the channel clean if we leave on the turn."

Redd looked eastward, measuring the cloud wall. "She'll give us rain, not a gale." He smiled slightly. "The Spaniards will see that same sky and think we've turned back. Let's prove them wrong."

Elias gave a short nod. "Aye, Captain."

For a breath, the air between them held mutual respect—two seamen reading the same water differently but recognizing the other's eye for it.

"Carry on," Redd said, and stepped to the quarterdeck.

The first drops fell as Grey crossed to the helm. The crew murmured about silver and stormlight; someone swore they could already smell the sugar cargo from leagues away.

He said nothing to cool them. Words wouldn't reach them now—not while the promise of fortune still burned brighter than caution.

He touched the serpent-and-anchor ring, the metal warm from his skin.

Locke's voice came as clear as surf in memory: *Fairness keeps a crew. Fear only borrows them.*

He looked toward Redd, standing tall in the gathering wind, and knew the truth of it.

Borrowed or not, they were his crew now.

Thunder rolled again, closer this time—like distant guns.

Elias turned his face into the wind and called, "Mr. Delgado—hands to braces! Ready her for sea."

Nico's answer came sharp and steady: "Aye, sir."

Lines ran. Canvas bloomed, dark against the gray sky. *The Sable Wraith* leaned into the tide, her bow pointing toward the open water where rumor and weather waited together.

Grey kept one hand on the rail, eyes fixed on the horizon. Where Locke had taught through fairness, Redd taught through risk. Either way, the sea would decide which lesson held.

CHAPTER THREE

The Hunt

*T*he *Sable Wraith* slipped from Nassau harbor under the fading light of evening, her black hull cutting through the channel while the sun sank behind the palms. Lanterns along the quay winked out one by one. By the time the last reef bell sounded, she was clear of the shoals and heading south-by-west into open water. Behind her, the island burned orange on the horizon; ahead, the Caicos Passage waited under a low bank of cloud.

The wind came steady out of the east-northeast, filling her canvas in long breaths. The ship leaned into it like a beast glad to be moving. On deck, Elias Grey moved quietly among the men—checking lashings, feeling the helm's response, gauging how the ship carried herself.

"Keep her two points south-by-west," he said, one hand on the rail.

The quartermaster eased the wheel; the compass card steadied.

Redd stood above on the quarterdeck, glass tucked under his arm, the sea wind combing through the loose strands of his hair. Whatever swagger Nassau lent him ashore, he left it there. At sea he was composed, sober, watching wind and cloud as if measuring an opponent's reach.

"Hold that line," he said.

"Aye, Captain."

The men settled into their night rhythm—fewer words, steadier motion. Nico carried the work through the deck like current through wire: sharp commands, no waste. His whistle rose once, high and thin, and the braces came taut. The ship's creak and hiss turned rhythmic, purposeful.

By the time the stars came out, Nassau was gone behind a haze of heat and memory. The moon rose small and white, throwing a pale road across the water. Squalls wandered the horizon, flashing now and again like distant guns. The night felt close, humid, thick with waiting.

Shortly after midnight, the mistake came. Tom Barlow—a greenhand big enough to move a barrel by himself but still clumsy as a shore ox—took hold of the wrong fall when the wind freshened. The brace jerked, a block swung wild, and a line snapped against the deck like a whip.

Redd was there in three strides. He caught the nearest rope-end and struck the boy once, flat and quick. "Watch your hands," he said—voice even, not cruel. "This ship keeps her own account."

Barlow froze, wide-eyed.

Elias stepped in, tone calm but firm. "Re-reeve it as taught. Slowly."

The boy's fingers trembled, then steadied. Pull, take, turn, hitch—the pattern came back.

"Belay," Elias said. "Mr. Delgado, check his hitch."

Nico tugged it, nodded. "Holds, sir."

Redd watched the scene without a word, then turned aft. The matter was done. The crew exhaled together—soundless but felt.

Elias crouched beside the boy, examining the welt on his hand. "Fear makes clumsy sailors," he said quietly. "Steady hands keep you alive."

"Yes, sir," Barlow whispered.

"Good. Go on."

The rest of the night passed under heavy clouds and the smell of rain. *The Wraith* ran silent—ports closed, powder double-wrapped, guns primed and lashed. Elias shifted men at the braces for quick reefing, posted a lookout in the cross-trees, and kept the surgeon topside for weather or worse.

Around midnight the lookout called softly from aloft. "Lanterns—three points off the port bow."

Elias climbed halfway to the quarterdeck, eyes narrowing into the wind. Far off, three faint lights pulsed in a line: escorts, running north under convoy sail. Too distant to hear, close enough to smell the danger of them.

Redd joined him at the rail, glass raised. The lights wavered through mist. "Convoy frigates," he said. "Running heavy. They'll make for the Channel before daylight."

Elias studied their angle. "If we keep low to the wind, they'll never catch scent of us."

Redd's grin was quick, wolfish. "Then we'll slip their teeth. South another two points, Mr. Grey—quiet as thieves."

The Wraith eased down into shadow. Canvas muted, lanterns doused, she became a darker shape within the dark—wind and purpose alone. The escorts passed like ghosts across their bow, blind to what hunted behind them. When their lights vanished into haze, Redd exhaled once, satisfied.

"Now," he murmured. "Let's find the one they were guarding."

Toward dawn the wind eased, veering a fraction north. Flotsam drifted by in the half-light—a crate-slat, a lemon peel, a torn scrap of sailcloth marked with a Spanish hand. Convoy debris.

"Convoy water," Elias said, watching the pieces turn in the swell.

Redd appeared beside him, glass raised. "They're out here, then."

Elias pointed to the faint pull of current curling from the southeast. "They're running up from Cartagena. If we hold this course, we'll meet them in open light."

Redd nodded. "South-by-east, then—to keep our weather gauge."

"Aye, Captain."

The Wraith heeled slightly as she answered the wheel. Morning bled up from the horizon—a dull silver glow through thin rain. The men moved quieter than usual, each one aware that silence has its own kind of superstition.

By first light the sky broke into pale streaks. The lookout's call came thin and sure: "Sail leeward—fine on the bow!"

Redd's glass went up instantly. Elias didn't bother; he watched the lookout's lean. A man leaning forward meant truth, not hope.

"Can you mark it?" Redd asked.

"Square-rigged, small," Elias said. "Deep in the water—heavy."

Redd adjusted the glass. "Could be our sugar brig. Let's see if she likes company."

He lowered the glass, voice low but clear. "Mr. Voss, ready the larboard guns. Ports closed. Mr. Peck, grapples coiled but out of sight. Mr. Delgado, trim her for a chase."

Orders moved through the ship like pulses. Lines tightened, hands braced, *The Wraith* packing her weight into speed. Elias felt the hull hum underfoot—not excitement exactly, but the live energy of purpose.

The wind freshened with the sunrise, drawing fine threads of spray from the bow. Far ahead, the brig's hull took shape: salt-crusted, paint faded, sails patched and heavy. No gunports open. She moved like a tired beast too slow to hide.

"Range?" Redd asked.

"Two cables," Elias said. "She's running but not fighting."

Redd's mouth curved. "Then we'll wake her gently."

He raised his glass once more, scanning the rim of sea behind the brig. Nothing moved there but light and haze. "No sign of her escorts," he said, almost to himself. "They've strayed north, chasing phantoms out of Nassau. Didn't think we'd come from behind."

Elias kept his voice neutral. "If they're smart, they'll be doubling back."

"Then let's finish before they remember their duty." Redd's tone stayed easy, confident. He raised his hand, palm down. "Mr. Grey—bring her on the stern quarter."

The brig's wake ran ragged to the northwest, her course bending toward the Bahama Channel. Grey studied the angle, gauging drift and wind, then gave the adjustment. "North-by-west, a half point. Helm to it."

The Wraith swung through the wind, falling neatly into the Spaniard's wake, her bow now pointing north with the rising sun. The air thickened with drizzle and the sharp tang of powder readied in the hold. Men stood by their guns, breath clouding the chill dawn air.

"Ports down on my word," Redd said, voice barely above a whisper. "One broadside to quiet her courage—then we ask for her manners."

Elias's hand rested lightly on the rail. "Aye, Captain."

He looked ahead at the brig—her white flag still furled, her crew small shapes moving in panic or prayer. He thought of Locke for half a heartbeat—of Cartagena and the sea that remembers everything.

"Range, one cable!" came the call.

Redd lifted his hand.

"Now," he said.

Elias's voice carried through wind and rain, even and final. "Ports down!"

Wood slammed open. *The Wraith's* larboard guns bellowed in perfect rhythm—thunder rolling over water that already smelled of consequence.

CHAPTER FOUR

The Devil's Share

*T*he *Sable Wraith* fired as one body, her whole frame kicking against the recoil. The deck leapt under Elias's boots; heat and sound slammed the air flat. Salt and powder mingled as the broadside tore through the brig's sterncastle.

Splinters and iron rained back in a golden spray. The Spanish ship lurched, her mainmast shuddering as stays parted with a snap like rifle fire. Through the smoke Elias caught a glimpse—men scattering, one hurled into the scuppers, another clawing at a shattered gun.

"Run out! Sponge and load!" Nico's voice cut through the roar.

Elias steadied himself by the rail, eyes on the target. The brig yawed hard to larboard, her sails hanging like torn curtains.

Then, within the smoke, a white square began to climb a broken spar. The flag jerked, caught wind, and hung there limp and pleading.

"She's surrendering!" Nico called.

"Hold fire!" Elias answered.

The crew froze mid-motion, adrenaline still humming in their bones. Across the gap, the Spanish ship sagged and smoked, her stern torn open to daylight.

Redd lowered his glass, smile thin and sharp. "No escorts yet," he said. "Good."

He turned, voice calm as the sea beneath them. "Boarding party—armed. Take your powder, Mr. Grey."

Elias met his eye, then nodded once. Duty. Always duty.

Hooks flew, lines went taut, and the two hulls kissed with a dull groan. Redd crossed first, pistol already in hand. Elias followed with Nico and ten men, boards shaking under their weight.

The brig listed badly; her deck was a field of splinters and half-buried shot. Sugar dust mixed with smoke—a strange sweetness in the air.

Men waited by the mainmast—twenty maybe, ragged, faces gray beneath soot. One wore a weathered naval coat with tarnished braid at the cuffs. He stepped forward, hat in hand, dignity unbroken.

"Señor," he said, voice careful, English marked by education. "We surrender. We serve the Crown—cargo for Havana."

Redd studied him. "You serve the Crown." He glanced toward the open hatch where the glint of silver leaked through torn canvas. "I serve survival."

The Spaniard inclined his head slightly. "Then you are already dead, Captain. Men without God live by moments."

Redd's eyes cooled. "Then let's make the most of this one."

He gestured with his pistol. "Hands to the mast. We leave no witnesses."

His men moved without hesitation, stripping knives and pistols from those who still wore them. The Spaniards obeyed—beaten but proud—some crossing themselves, one clutching a rosary until his knuckles whitened.

Elias stepped closer. "Captain," he said quietly, steel beneath the calm. "They're unarmed. The fight's done. There's no honor in this."

Redd didn't turn. "Honor?" he said. "They'd hang us for less than today."

"Then let them hang us for battle," Elias said, "not for murder."

That made Redd face him—quick, sharp, eyes narrowing. His voice came hard and clipped. "Enough, Grey. You'll question me on my own deck next? I'm not asking for sermons."

He motioned to the gunner, pistol still steady. "Mercy's the Devil's share, boy. Leave it to priests."

The words landed like a slap. Elias started to speak, but Redd's hand had already dropped in signal.

The first shot cracked through the smoke—small, almost delicate after the thunder of the guns. The second followed before the first echo died. Men folded where they stood.

The Spaniard in the naval coat stayed upright a heartbeat longer, meeting Elias's eyes across the space between them. No hatred there—only weary disbelief. He coughed once, dark blood blooming across the collar of his coat, then sagged to his knees and fell forward.

Powder smoke rolled low and thick, carrying the bittersweet of burned sugar. The sea around them went very still.

Redd holstered his pistol. "Strip her hold," he said, tone all business. "Silver, sugar, letters. Then scuttle her."

Men moved. Crates thudded, coins clinked into canvas. Nico worked mechanically, face ashen. Elias forced himself to help—muscle and memory taking over where thought failed. The deck was slick; the air, heavy with salt and iron.

"Magazine's dry, Captain," the gunner called from below. "Forward bulkhead's split."

Redd nodded once. "Fetch a keg. Lay a line to the hatch. We'll light her before we disembark."

The gunner returned with a small powder keg and a coil of match. He trailed a narrow line through the wreck, the powder hissing softly as it settled into the cracks. The smell of it made the air taste metallic.

"Ready," the gunner said.

Redd struck a match on his belt buckle, the tiny flame bright in the gray morning. He touched it to the powder and watched it catch, crawling toward the hatch.

"Back to the *Wraith*," he ordered.

They crossed quickly, men leaping the narrow gap one by one. Elias was last. As he stepped onto his own deck, he turned to see smoke curling from the brig's broken belly.

A muffled thump—then a rolling, thunder-deep roar. The hull split; flame and debris burst upward, raining back in splinters and spray. The ship's spine folded. For a breath she hung there, then slid beneath the surface.

The sea closed—white first, then red, then calm.

Redd broke the silence. "Clean your weapons. Salt eats steel faster than guilt."

The men obeyed without a word, cloths rasping over pistols and blades.

Elias wiped his own pistol, though he had not fired a shot. Each pass slowed, the motion mechanical, penitent. His hands shook though the deck did not.

He looked toward the smoke fading across the water. Nothing left—no masts, no flag, no proof she'd ever been.

"Mercy earns consequence," he said under his breath. The words felt smaller now, worn thin.

Only the steady sound of rags on metal answered him—the last prayer left aboard.

The Wraith came about slowly, her wake cutting through drifting ash as the morning sun burned the smoke to gold.

CHAPTER FIVE

Ash and Wine

The tavern breathed heat and noise. Lamplight slicked across wet tables; rum ran like a river; dice clattered in a roar that never quite turned into song. The Widow's Glass was half ship, half den—tar-stained beams, a ceiling so low a tall man could rake it with his knuckles, and a cracked mirror behind the counter that made the whole room look doubled: twice the men, twice the gold, twice the ghosts.

The crew of *The Wraith* filled it to the rafters. Silver flashed under lanterns, coins skittered, a knife thunked into wood and stayed humming there. Laughter came hard and bright, the kind men use to drown out yesterday.

A fiddler fought his instrument in the corner and lost. Someone started a sea-ditty and forgot the end of every line.

Elias sat against the far wall with a single cup that hadn't moved. He watched the room as if it were weather—something that would pass if he kept still long enough. The smell was salt, smoke, wet wool, and cheap molasses. His hands were clean. His pistol, back in the cabin, was clean too. The cloth had come away black, then gray, then clean—and none of it had helped.

Nico slid onto the bench beside him, shoulders damp with the night. A splash of rum climbed the side of his cup and tipped back again with the motion of the crowd.

"They'll drink till dawn," he said without looking, as if they were discussing the tide.

"So they won't have to remember what we did today," Elias said.

Nico's mouth twitched. "You eat?"

"Not hungry."

"Me neither."

Across the room, Redd held court at the largest table, the ship's quartermaster stacking coins in bright towers while men slapped his shoulders for luck. Redd wore laughter like an officer's sash. Each time he raised his cup the room grew louder, as if the sound started in him and ran outward.

He looked up once and found Elias through the press. The smile didn't slip, but the angle of it changed.

He said something to the men around him, then stood. The crowd parted without needing to be told.

He came like weather too—pressure dropping with every step. When he reached Elias's table he set his cup down hard enough to wake it.

"You drink like a priest at a hanging," Redd said, voice low but cutting through the noise. "Lift a cup—we've earned it."

Elias didn't rise to meet him. He lifted his eyes instead, and it felt like standing up. "You earned it, Captain. I kept count."

Redd laughed—short as a blade drawn and shown. The nearest tables shifted; men turned at their elbows, ears angling without guilt. The fiddler stopped pretending to win his song.

Redd slid onto the bench opposite. Lantern light built a wobbling wall of gold between them. "Still brooding over a few Spaniards?" he asked, light as you please.

Elias let the noise move around them and then past. "You call it victory," he said. "I call it slaughter."

Redd's smile thinned. "You forget what Locke taught you—mercy gets men killed."

"Locke taught that command is burden, not license."

"He taught poetry," Redd said, the words drying as they left his mouth. "And poetry got him dead. If he'd fought like me, he'd still be breathing."

The name hung there like a bell struck and held. Behind Redd, someone laughed too loudly at nothing. Nico's hand tightened on his cup until the pewter groaned.

Elias lowered his voice until it felt like it sat at the bottom of the room. "You mistake cruelty for strength," he said. "It's the coward's mask."

Chairs creaked but didn't move. The mirror behind the counter caught the two of them and broke them into pieces—Redd in shards of gold and shadow, Elias a thin dark line.

Redd leaned forward until the lantern edge found the scar along his jaw. "Careful, lad."

"You'll hang men for less than the truth," Elias said.

For a heartbeat, steel lived in the air between them. Redd's right hand eased from his cup to the table; Elias's fingers flattened—empty and ready—the same gesture sailors use before a squall.

Rain began tapping the shutters then—soft, steady, the sound of a drum heard from a hill away.

Redd exhaled, and with the breath he let out his smile again. He wasn't amused so much as choosing to be. "There he is," he said softly. "The little captain the boys whisper about when they get pious."

He lifted his cup and leaned in until the words were for Elias alone. "You think you're a captain?" His breath smelled of good rum and bad resolve. "Then act like one."

He rose before Elias could answer. The moment broke like glass. Redd turned back to the room and held his cup high. "To *The Wraith!*"

The roar came greedy and grateful. Benches jumped; the knife in the table thrummed again. Laughter flooded the corners and drove out the last of the quiet. Someone threw a handful of silver, and men swore and scrambled as coins rang against wood and bone.

Elias picked up his cup because habit is its own chain. He touched it to his lips and let the rum set his mouth on fire without swallowing more than a drop.

Nico watched Redd's back with a look people save for churches—the fury you can only feel when you've been taught better. "He doesn't mean it, about Locke," he said. "Not like that."

Elias kept his eyes on the lantern, which flickered as if it were considering going out. "He means it enough."

"They'll call you the priest," Nico said, half warning, half promise.

"They already do," Elias said, and set the cup down where it wouldn't spill.

The room tried to become a song again and failed. Dice rattled. A man with silver on his tongue announced he could buy Nassau twice over and drink it dry. The mirror made him emperor of a kingdom of stain and smoke.

Redd returned to his table and turned the tide by will alone. He leaned into a story that grew with each hand gesture; men bent toward him as if he were wind and they were candles. He laughed at the right moment, and the room lifted. He tilted the next roll of bones with his smile. He won because the house always belongs to men like him—until it burns.

Elias waited for his breath to steady and found it wasn't coming back the way it used to. He looked at Nico. "Go sleep," he said. "Or pray. Both cost less than this."

Nico snorted. "Prayers don't work for men like him."

"They're not for him."

A fight tried to start across the room—a shove that drew a curse that drew a fist. It blew out in the next cheer like a match in gusty weather. The tavern had no room for another kind of violence tonight; there wasn't oxygen for it.

Redd's eyes cut over once more, checking the place where he'd left Elias, and saw him still there. He tipped his cup in a salute that could have meant anything, then turned back to his court.

Elias stood. The bench groaned in relief. Nico rose with him but didn't follow.

"You going?" he asked.

"Out," Elias said.

"The rain's come in."

"I know."

He crossed the room the way a man wades into surf—expecting the drag and leaning against it. Shoulders brushed him; hands clapped the back of his coat out of habit more than affection. The door fought him and then let him through.

Outside, Nassau's night had turned to smeared ink. Rain slicked the alley stones and turned gutter water to silver where lantern light found it. Laughter leaked through plank walls and ran along puddles until it thinned into the hiss of the tide.

He stood beneath the tavern's overhang and breathed until the rum-smell faded from his mouth. Across the street, a woman tipped a bucket and sent a sheet of water off a stoop; the splash came back as coins somewhere behind him landed on wood. The church bell—somewhere uphill and unwilling—counted the hour in a slow, stubborn measure.

He looked once through the window as if checking a compass. Redd sat facing the room again, lamplight painting him in bars of gold and shadow. The mirror behind him made two Redds, then four, then the whole crowd of him, multiplied into a truth the island preferred.

Elias turned his collar up and stepped into the rain. It found the back of his neck and rubbed salt into it. He walked toward the harbor without hurry, boots clipping a rhythm he didn't have to think about. His reflection broke and healed in every puddle.

Down at the quay, *The Wraith* lay black and patient against a smear of lightning far offshore. Her lines were fixed, her lanterns low—a creature asleep but dangerous in sleep. He could see the curve of her rail and the places men had gripped it until the grain shone. He could have found his place blindfolded.

He didn't go aboard. He stood with the stink of rope and wet wood and let the night take the sound of the tavern away piece by piece until only the rain and the tide remained. Somewhere behind him a bottle shattered. Somewhere ahead of him a gull woke and decided against it.

You think you're a captain? Redd's voice said again in his ear, and he understood it for what it was—not a taunt, but a dare.

Respect and obedience had parted company in that room. One had left quietly without paying. The other would settle its account soon enough.

He stayed until the bell counted again. Then he turned back toward the lights, because dawn always insists—and men must face whoever they become in it.

Chapter Six

The Whispering Crew

Rain found the ship first.

It came soft and steady out of a slate-gray sky, drumming on the tarred planks in a rhythm the crew could measure their breath by. *The Wraith* lay at anchor just outside the harbor mouth, her guns run in, her decks slick and shining. Lanterns swung low, their light caught in the rigging like tired stars.

Below, the air was close and thick with damp rope and salt pork. Men spoke in half-voices; laughter came in fragments that didn't last. The smell of wet hemp and bilge water clung to everything. A few played dice on an overturned cask, the click of bone a metronome for the rain above. Others lay in their hammocks, eyes open, staring at nothing.

In the small aftercabin, Elias sat alone, lamplight puddled across the map he wasn't reading. The rain overhead sounded like distant drums—patient, deliberate. Now and then, a gust rattled the stern windows, and drops found their way through the seams. He didn't move to stop them. The water ran across the chart, blurring coastlines he already knew by heart.

He thought of Locke—of the man's voice before battle, steady and measured. *A crew divided never sails far.* The words came like a tide, uninvited but familiar.

Somewhere forward, the murmur of men rose and fell again—a ripple of sound moving through a ship too quiet for comfort.

In the half-light of the gun deck, the younger sailors spoke as if the rain could carry their words away.

"Aye. Called him a butcher."

Another spat into the scupper. "Then he's a fool. Redd breaks fools."

A third, barely older than the boy they'd buried at sea months ago, shook his head. "He's got right on his side. The priest knows what he's about."

That word—*priest*—hung in the air like smoke. No one liked it, but no one stopped it either.

"They'll keelhaul him next," muttered a man from his hammock. "Redd don't forgive saints."

"You think Redd's wrong?" the younger one asked.

Silence answered him. The timbers creaked, the rain ticking above. Then someone said it, quiet but clear: "If Grey'd been captain, those Spaniards would still breathe."

A pause.

"Then we'd all be dead," another said, sharper.

The stillness that followed was heavier than shouting.

Nico stepped from the shadows near the powder room, sleeves rolled, face unreadable. "Watch your mouth," he said.

The men turned; nobody moved.

The one who'd spoken grinned thinly. "Aye, priest's boy. Go pray it clean."

Nico hit him before the words finished leaving his mouth. A short, flat sound—the kind of strike that means business, not anger. The man staggered, swung back, and caught Nico across the cheek. Hammocks rocked; dice scattered.

It lasted only seconds. When it was over, both were bleeding from somewhere, both breathing hard. The others stared at the deck boards.

Nico wiped his mouth with the back of his hand. "You speak his name," he said, low, almost calm, "you speak it with respect."

No one answered. The rain filled the silence—steady and patient as judgment.

— ⚓ —

In his cabin, Elias felt it start—the thud, the muffled curse, the way a ship changes tone when fists find timber. He didn't rise. The oil in the lamp trembled with each blow. Then it was over, and the sound of the rain came back like nothing had happened.

He leaned back, eyes on the deck beams. He knew exactly what it was, and what it meant.

Leadership, he thought, wasn't command. It wasn't barked orders or a captain's temper. It was what men did when they thought you weren't listening.

The rain softened, became whisper instead of drum. He could smell wet oak and gun oil, the ghost of smoke still in the planks.

Belief, once spoken aloud, becomes rebellion.

He said Locke's words under his breath. "A crew divided never sails far."

It didn't sound like warning anymore. It sounded like prophecy.

Later, the deck was quiet again. The rain tapered to drizzle, a thin silver sheen running off the scuppers. Nico stood by the rail, knuckles swelling purple, looking out into the dark.

Elias joined him without a word. They stood side by side, faces turned toward the harbor lights flickering far off like candles behind glass.

"He won't forget," Elias said.

"I don't care," Nico answered.

"You should."

Elias looked at the boy's hands. Blood mixed with rain along the knuckles and slid away into the sea.

Lightning flared somewhere beyond the horizon—far, faint, as if deciding whether to come closer. *The Wraith* creaked under the soft push of the tide, restless even at anchor.

Neither man spoke again. The rain began anew—gentle and endless—drumming out the seconds until dawn.

CHAPTER SEVEN

The Captain's Measure

The summons came in Redd's careful hand, neat as a ledger line: *Officers to dine in the great cabin at the first bell of evening.* No flourish, no threat—the steadiness of it did the work.

By the time Elias reached the corridor, the rain had thinned to mist. The ship ticked and settled on her anchor line, lantern light running thin along the boards. Nico waited by the door with his arms behind his back, a bruise yellowing along the ridge of his cheekbone.

"He means to measure us tonight," Nico said softly.

"He's already weighed us," Elias answered, and pushed the latch.

Redd's great cabin glowed warm as a hearth. The maps were cleared from the table; waxed cloth folded and stowed. Silver gleamed under the lanterns—plates that had seen less food than pride, a row of cut-crystal cups that caught the light and threw it back in fractured stars. The air smelled of lamp oil and wine and beeswax, a clean scent meant to make men forget salt and powder.

"Mr. Grey." Redd rose from the head of the table with a smile that fit like a uniform. "Mr. Voss, Mr. Peck. Sit. Eat."

They took their places without scraping chairs. Nico remained near the bulkhead, a shadow with watchful eyes.

Redd poured the wine himself, slow and generous, the cut crystal blushing dark. "Nassau has suddenly discovered it owes us favors," he said lightly. "Merchants climb like crabs to shake our hands. Disgusting, really." He raised his cup in mock solemnity to the absurdity of it. The others obliged him with thin smiles.

Bread came, then stew, then a platter of fish slick with lemon and butter. Conversation scraped along the surface: a sail split and mended; a cask of beef turned sour and pitched; a merchant who tried to pay a debt in

Dominican sugar that had seen too much sea. Laughter landed three beats late and didn't linger.

Halfway through the fish, Redd leaned back and reached for a covered chart. He folded the cloth like a magician revealing nothing dangerous at all, only lines and latitude.

"Work," he said, pleasant as a schoolmaster. He set a finger on the chart and tapped once. "A French merchant brig, two days north-by-east. Small crew, fat hull. Paper says she's running for Martinique."

Peck shifted. Voss cleared his throat as if dislodging a thorn. No one mentioned the white flag that had climbed and failed two days past; no one spoke the word *Spanish* as if a syllable could call ghosts into a well-lit room.

Redd traced the route with a thumb. "She takes the edge of the trades to save water. We'll catch her here, weather permitting, or here if she has more courage than charts." He looked up, eyes bright. "She's no treasure ship—granted. But a prize is a prize, and honest work is good for men with idle hands. We sail at dawn."

Elias studied the inked coast, then the neat circle Redd's thumb had polished on the compass rose. His voice stayed mild. "Merchantmen carry families sometimes. Not soldiers."

Redd's smile didn't falter. "Then they shouldn't sail under another man's flag." He set down the compass with a little click, a decision rounding out. "Besides, there's no mention of passengers in the letters."

"Letters leave out what doesn't pay," Voss said, and wished he hadn't—the words hanging like damp laundry. "Spoken like a man who's been paid late," Redd teased. "Eat, Mr. Voss. You're pale."

They made a show of eating. The ship creaked, the harbor murmured, a gull called once as if to test the evening.

When the plates had been cleared to the sideboards, Redd stood with his cup. "Enough civility." His tone warmed by a degree that felt deliberate. "To *The Wraith*," he said, raising the glass, "and to men unafraid to dirty their hands."

Peck lifted his cup. Voss lifted his. Nico didn't move. Elias raised his without drinking.

"Clean hands," Elias said, almost conversationally, "are rarer than honest men."

The sentence landed like a knife set point-down on a tabletop—a simple touch, the threat in what might follow. The ship seemed to hold her breath.

Voss swallowed. Peck coughed into his sleeve. The lamplight hissed in the wick.

Redd didn't blink. Then he did, once, slowly, as if clearing grit from his eye. "You saying mine aren't clean, Mr. Grey?" His voice had lost nothing of its calm; only the shape of it had sharpened.

"I'm saying they're honest," Elias answered. He set his cup down gently.

For a moment Redd's face emptied, the smile gone without anything to take its place. Then he laughed—a full, round sound that went on two beats too long and filled the cabin like smoke.

"God save me from philosophers," he said, when the laugh had drained to a grin. He topped his own cup, then Voss's and Peck's, spilling a red thread on the table and not wiping it. "Drink, all of you. Work makes men simple, and I prefer simple men before a sail."

They drank. Elias did not. He let the wine touch his lip and darken it and set the cup back again, a ring of red left on the polished wood.

Redd sat, elbows on the chair arms, fingertips together, studying Elias as if measuring him for a coat. "You'll have the morning watch," he said finally. "Take her out on the first wind. I want canvas high and clean and no squeal in the blocks. Mr. Peck, look to the powder; dry as a sermon. Mr. Voss, settle the shares with the men tonight so nobody invents mathematics at sea."

"Aye," they answered, grateful for instructions that made them smaller and safer.

The rest of the meal continued as meals do when danger has been named and set aside by force: bread torn, knives laid down carefully, the clink of spoons a little too loud. Redd told a brief story about a Dutchman in Curaçao who wept over a bolt of ruined silk; Peck forced a laugh at the proper place; Voss nodded at nothing.

At last the plates were cleared and the wine had dwindled. The officers rose on the gentle cue of Redd's hands opening over the table. Chairs pushed back on a softened scrape, heads dipped, duty regained its proper shape.

"Sleep, gentlemen," Redd said, standing with them. "Tomorrow we are honest sailors again."

Voss murmured something like thanks and escaped. Peck followed, bobbing his head toward the chart as if the lines might bless him. Nico stayed a pace behind Elias as they reached the door.

"Mr. Grey," Redd said.

Elias paused with his hand on the latch and turned back.

"You should sleep," Redd said pleasantly. "Tomorrow will be long."

"Aye, Captain."

Redd watched him a measure longer, smiling with everything except his eyes. "See you at the helm at dawn."

The corridor outside felt cooler, the air less perfumed. The ship breathed there, beams easing as the tide turned. From the stern skylight a square of night showed rigging in black strokes against a bruised sky. Far off beyond the harbor, lightning stitched a white seam along the horizon and let it fade.

Nico let the silence carry them to the ladder well before he spoke. "He heard you," he said.

"He was meant to," Elias replied.

"Peck heard you. Voss too."

"Good." Elias kept walking. "Better they decide what they'll be before the sea asks it of them."

On deck the mist had a taste of iron. The harbor lights moved in a slow sway as small boats came and went—dark shapes with red lanterns, voices carried thinly and broken by water. Sailcloth, furled and tied neat, dripped with the last of the rain. *The Wraith's* lines hummed now and then as a stray puff found them.

Elias crossed to the rail and set his palm on the wet elm. The sea slapped the hull in a patient rhythm, the ship's heartbeat matching it. From here, Redd's cabin was a warm rectangle of gold sternward; a figure moved through it, then vanished—the captain's shadow cutting and joining the light.

"You'll take the morning watch," Nico said, as if it needed saying.

"I will."

"You'll take us out clean."

"If the wind's honest."

Nico's bruised knuckles flexed and settled. "He'll test you again."

Elias kept his gaze on the horizon where the lightning stitched and unstitched the sky. "He can keep testing. The sea has the final say."

A small laugh escaped Nico, bitter and fond at once. "Locke would've liked that."

"Locke had better lines," Elias said.

The wind shifted a finger's width, tugging at the loose hair at his temple. He felt the change—a copper tang, the hush that comes before weather sets its hand on a ship. "Get what sleep you can."

"And you?"

"I'll borrow some from the deck."

Nico hesitated, then nodded and left him there.

He stood until the bell struck the hour—a single, patient note that wandered out over the water and came back thinner. The lanterns along the quay burned small and stubborn; far out, the reef threw back a pale line where the swell shouldered it. The rigging whispered as if talking in its sleep.

Behind him, in the quiet cabin, laughter rose once more and stopped as if pinched. He didn't turn. Dawn would come with its usual certainty; men would stand where they were told; sails would climb; the ship would lean into whatever future the weather had seen fit to bring.

He ran a thumb along the rail, and it came away slick and clean. The night smelled of rain and iron and the work to come. He breathed it in and let it rest there.

Battle lines had been drawn without a blade. Courtesy covered them for now like a fine cloth over a loaded table. When it lifted, there'd be no confusion about who sat where.

Elias looked once more at the horizon. Lightning answered by lighting the world to bone, then leaving it dark again. He nodded to no one, and the sea—as ever—kept her own counsel.

CHAPTER EIGHT

Into the Storm

B efore dawn the sky came down to meet the water and wouldn't lift. Heat pressed in behind it, metallic on the tongue, and the smell of rain lay over the harbor like a sheet.

Nassau slept in smudged lanterns and the whisper of small boats turning lazily on their painters. The reef beyond the mouth flickered—lightning sketching its teeth in quick white lines. The second bell sounded thin and patient. No dogs barked.

Redd had given the order the night before: *first tide, weather be damned.* So *The Wraith* moved like a man waking from a hard dream—deliberate, making no noise it didn't need to make. Lines came in hand over hand, wet and heavy; the anchor chain rose link by link out of black water, weeping. Men spoke in half-voices because the air felt close enough to bruise.

Elias stood by the gangway and watched the sky stutter to life beyond the reef. Lightning walked there like a man with somewhere to be. He felt the taste of copper behind his teeth and the old, clean space open in him that a storm always opened—the one that made room for what comes next.

"Hands to stations," Nico called, whistle high and thin. "Light and quiet. Heave—and—heave."

The Wraith turned her head to the harbor mouth. Sails climbed—dark wings against a bruised ceiling; canvas thudded, took wind, and drew. The ship leaned as if relieved to be herself again. Rain found the deck in big, spaced drops that sounded like thrown pebbles.

Redd's silhouette took the quarterdeck, steady as a carved figurehead. "North-by-east," he called down.

"North-by-east," Elias answered from the helm. The wheel moved under his hands like it was breathing. The words felt like a sentence pronounced, not an order given.

They passed the last quay light. The mouth narrowed. On the far side, the reef blinked in and out with each lightning stitch. The harbor fell astern with a sigh—a city of oil lamps fading to a few stubborn stars.

Beyond the reef, the sea rose in long, muscular swells. Wind came in fists. Rain thickened into sheets that slanted under the force of it, drumming the planks, watering the men's eyes. Bare feet slid; hands found rope; curses blew away clean as soon as they were born.

"Reef the fore!" Redd shouted. "Ease the main—two hands on the lee braces—hold—now!"

His voice threaded the weather like a needle through canvas. The crew moved with it—not graceful, but true—muscle memory, trust in timber and in each other. *The Wraith* took the reefing without complaint, shook her shoulders, and drove on.

Spray cut Elias's face and tasted of iron. He leaned into the wheel and felt the ship talk to him—the under-tug of the swell, the shudder of a gust shouldering the main, the minute lag between order and obedience.

Locke's voice came the way old voices do at sea—uninvited and exact. *Mercy's a choice, lad. Choose it, and the sea will judge the rest.*

He didn't answer. He'd already chosen. The sea could do her work.

A white fork tore the horizon open, turning night to bone. For a heart-beat the world had hard edges: rigging black and perfect against a sky of hammered tin; Redd above with his coat snapping and his grin fixed like iron; Nico below, mouth open on a command that the thunder swallowed whole.

Then the dark dropped back in, deeper for the moment of exposure. Thunder rolled over them like cannon fire from a line of ships unseen, each report chasing the last until the sound seemed to circle the world and come back.

"Hold her to it!" Elias called, though his voice barely reached Nico at the lee rail.

"Aye!" Nico threw back, teeth white in the gloom.

The reef fell away on the quarter. Open water took them whole. *The Wraith* leaned, accepted the weight, and ran—bow throwing gray water in sheets that flashed and vanished; sails full and roaring, edges humming like struck wire. The compass card steadied on its mark; the wheel spoke in Elias's palms. He set his jaw and gave the storm what it asked.

Lightning stitched the horizon again, wider, nearer. Thunder followed like the roll of guns across calm water. The rain lost its shape and became a world.

"Stand by your lines," Redd called, calm at the center. "No slack, no squeal. Let her breathe."

Elias glanced up once. For a heartbeat the lightning had him: the captain cast in white, eyes bright with hunger, all edges, all intent. Elias looked away first and fixed on the feel of elm beneath his hands and the way the bow cut the next swell clean.

They ran like that until there was nothing left of Nassau but a taste of lamp soot and a memory of warm rain. Ahead, the storm widened to take them, and they went willingly into it—men and hull and canvas a single thing—because there was no other honest road.

The horizon flashed white, thunder rolling like gunfire, and the sea closed its hands around *The Wraith*.

CHAPTER NINE

The Prize

Morning scraped a dull edge across the sea, light leaking through a patched sky until the water took on the color of tarnished brass. The night's squall marched away to the east, muttering. Sails dripped. Rigging sang in short, tired notes.

Elias stood at the quarterdeck rail, glass to his eye. A single brig ran ahead—fat in the water, canvas patched, wake ragged. French colors lifted and sagged with each lazy swell.

Redd came up from below with a smile that showed teeth. "There's your prize," he said.

"A sugar brig by her lines," Elias answered, lowering the glass. "She's heavy."

"Then she won't run far. Mr. Peck, rouse your men. Mr. Voss, mind the shares will need tidying—think like a clerk now, or bleed like a fool later." Redd's grin sharpened. "Wake her."

"Aye," Peck called, already moving.

Elias stepped to the wheel. "Two points to windward on the forebrace," he called to Nico. "Shake a hand's breadth from the main, and keep the leeward sheets easy. We'll take the wind she can't carry."

Nico's whistle cut the morning. Lines thumped through blocks; men leaned and heaved. *The Wraith* answered at once—shoulders squaring, weight gathering underfoot, the long hum of speed rising through her bones. Water sheared off her bow in bright, torn sheets.

Ahead, the brig felt it. She clawed up more sail, hoisted staysails with no business in this air, and rolled for it. Her boom swung too wide; her deckhands stumbled with the strain.

"She's over-rigged for her weight," Elias said, almost to himself. "She'll yank the teeth from her own comb."

"Then we'll save her the barber," Redd said, amused.

Smoke puffed from the brig's waist. Not the galley—the wrong place. Elias watched the gray feather drift and curl. "They're lighting matches," he said. "Guns coming live."

"Good," Redd replied. "I hate a prize that doesn't introduce herself."

"Run out the larboard battery," Elias called down. "Powder tight, sponges wet. I want a clean first word."

Peck's gun crews moved with that miserable, beautiful calm that comes from practice and near misses. Worms and sponges went like clockwork. Breeching ropes were checked and kissed in instinct, not prayer. Powder monkeys hugged their charges like they were ferrying newborns.

"Range?" Redd asked.

"Two and a half cables," Elias said. "Closing."

The brig fired first—three shots, hurried and high. One splashed close enough to dust *The Wraith's* bow with spray. A cheer rose—quick, then cut short—from the brig's men.

"Hold," Elias said, watching the roll, feeling the timing in his knees. "Hold... now."

"Fire as she bears!" Peck roared.

The Wraith spoke with a stitched thunder, each gun thumping into the next. Smoke leapt and tore and laid down. The brig shuddered. One of her topmasts snapped like a stalk of cane; canvas went slack and snarled. Timber coughed splinters the size of knives.

"Reload!" Peck shouted. Powder hissed. Rammers thunked. Men moved the way men move when they want to live.

The brig's reply came closer, truer. A ball ripped across *The Wraith's* waist, spitting a comb of splinters. A gun captain clapped both hands to his throat and sat down without seeming to mean to. Blood found the seams and ran for the scuppers. Nico was there before anyone called, pressing a rag too small to a wound too large.

Elias braced and shifted the wheel—two points down, smooth and firm. *The Wraith* answered, the bow easing onto the brig's quarter, her guns falling in line like trained dogs.

"Steady," he murmured, mostly to himself. The ship felt alive beneath him—responsive, ready.

The next broadside tore through the brig's stern windows. Glass shattered; her wheel spun free.

"She's bleeding, Captain," Nico said from the braces, already back on his feet, rag red to the elbow.

"Then let her feel it," Redd answered, eyes bright.

The brig tried again—two guns barking doggedly, iron balls tripping along *The Wraith's* flank and skipping away. Elias barely blinked.

"Quarterdeck guns," he said. "Low. On the third roll."

They took the third roll and spoke. Iron kissed wood and water at once. The brig lurched as if her knees had been kicked out; her mainmast gave up the argument entirely and splashed into the sea, dragging rigging and hope with it.

Her return fire died with the mast. Smoke cleared in ragged breaths. Men on her deck—small and human again—hauled lines or let them go and couldn't decide which was worse.

"Enough," Elias said—not to Redd, not to Peck; maybe to the sea. "Stand by."

"Boarding party!" Redd drew his sword like a stage cue. "Grapples ready. Nico, on me. Mr. Grey, you'll lead."

"Aye," Elias said, because there was nothing else a man like him could say and still face the mirror later.

Hooks flew. Their teeth bit splinter and stayed. Lines went taut with a singing strain. The ships kissed harder than was polite—hull to hull, groaning.

Elias went over the rail with pistol and cutlass. The world shrank to the span of a deck and the length of an arm. The brig's planks were slick with sugar and rain and blood—a treacherous mix that stank like a kitchen that had learned grief.

French and Creole shouted at once, high and hot. Smoke lived at waist height; powder burned the tongue. A man with a boarding axe came at Elias sideways; Elias caught the haft on his cutlass and drove a boot into the man's knee. Something broke—wood or bone, it didn't matter—turning a lunge into a kneel. The butt of Elias's pistol found the man's temple and put him down clean.

Nico collided with another; both slid on the sugared deck. They rolled. An axe-blade skittered away to bite harmlessly at a scupper. Nico's elbow rose and fell twice; the other man went slack and leaking. Nico's breath sawed smoke.

A pistol cracked inches from Elias's ear—small and sharp—heat grazing his cheek. He turned with the motion, found the shooter, and cut—clean through the collarbone, a stroke meant to end the fight, not make a point. The man dropped without a word, blood dark against the slick deck. Elias didn't look twice. There were still others standing.

The fight was quick and ugly the way sea fights are when one side has already lost but refuses to know it. Boots slid. Blades clanged and clattered. Men grunted. Someone sobbed once and stopped.

It buckled fast. Two minutes, perhaps three—the measure of a prayer said poorly—and then a man with an officer's sash yanked it off and flung it down as if it burned. He tossed his sword next, hands raised, breath tearing at his chest. "Je rends! Je rends!" he shouted, hoarse. "Assez! Assez!" He looked for English and found enough. "We yield!"

A white cloth—somebody's shirt—went up the foremast. It hung there, soaked and tattered, honest in a way the day wasn't.

Silence fell the way noise does—sudden, total, with a weight that took a second to adjust to. Men froze where they stood, then remembered their lungs. The air smelled of sugar steam and iron and the last of the night's rain. The brig listed a little to port; water sloshed in corners that had never meant to hold it.

Elias wiped his blade on his coat's hem and didn't look at whether the blood was his. His chest pulled for air and found enough. Nico leaned in, knocked breath back into a lung that complained about it, and grinned without joy.

"Enough," Elias said again, and this time it had a place to land. "Secure the wounded first. Then the weapons."

"Aye," Nico said, already moving.

Redd crossed last, boots ringing, sword idle at his side, pistol dangling. He walked the length of the damage with a collector's eye and a butcher's appetite.

"A clean prize," he said brightly, like a host admiring his own table. "Quick and true. The sea loves bold men."

Cheering tried to gather and failed. A few throats offered thin noise and let it die. The rest panted and swallowed and looked where not looking would have been a lie.

Redd laughed. It started in a place that could have passed for happiness and kept going until it belonged somewhere else. The sound sat wrong in the smoke—too long, too loud, too pleased with itself.

Elias felt pride twist into a cold knot and then into nothing he had a name for. They had done it clean—trim and timing and the right iron in the right wood. He could have written it as a lesson: how to take a brig without breaking her back; how to leave canvas for towing; how to stop a fight before it turned ugly enough to be remembered. And still the air smelled like the Spanish master's collar—dark and wet.

"Secure the prisoners," he said, low.

"Oh," Redd said, turning the word like a coin, "we'll see to them." He clapped Elias on the shoulder hard enough to make the world jump and smiled into his face like a lantern held close. "You've earned a front-row seat, Mr. Grey. Let's see what surrender earns."

Elias held his gaze and said nothing. The French officer stood nearby with empty hands and dignity he hadn't had time to misplace, looking from one English face to another like a man learning a language on the last day of his life.

"Papers," Elias said to him, gentler than he meant. "*Cartes. Documents.*" The officer nodded quickly, grateful for any question that wasn't the last one a man hears.

"*Dans la cabine*—inside. Please."

Redd spread his hands. "Hear that? Inside. A civilized people." He glanced to Peck. "We'll read after. Guns to safe. Pikes away. We'll not skewer our property."

Peck nodded, wary. He'd heard Redd's jokes before. Men began to gather the wounded—from both sides—into sensible piles. Pistols were unloaded into a crate. Blades were herded into a bucket like eels. The white cloth hung still, no wind to move it—the only honest thing between both ships.

Nico returned, face set, hands steady despite the dried blood. "All done that needs doing for now," he said to Elias in a voice that didn't invite praise. Elias glanced once at *The Wraith* riding easy alongside, her lines humming, her deck already wiped clean of what had happened. He looked back at the brig—sugar and salt and blood and men who had done what men do when they're told to hold a deck against a storm with iron in it.

"Keep two hands with the wounded," he said. "Ours and theirs. Water first. Then bandage."

"Aye."

Redd's shadow crossed both of them. "You're sweet today," he said lightly. "Careful you don't rot." He tilted his head, listening to some music only he could hear. "Set the prisoners amidships," he told Peck, pleasant as wine. "Kneel them if they prefer prayer."

Peck glanced at Elias—an instinct, a treason, a plea—and then away. "Aye, Captain."

Elias's jaw tightened until it hurt. *We've won clean. Don't ruin it.* The thought was simple and had no path to the mouth that wouldn't cost too much, too soon.

Redd's smile stayed. "Come along," he said softly, almost kind. "You'll want to see this."

The deck creaked as men shifted and obeyed. The smoke thinned. The sun tried to make a promise it couldn't keep. The white cloth hung where a flag should, and the sea—as always—kept her counsel.

CHAPTER TEN

The Breaking Point

The rain came steady now, a gray sheet that softened the light but not the air. The captured brig rolled gently against her lines, deck tilting to the slow rhythm of the sea. Blood and sugar had slicked the planks; the smell was thick enough to taste. The prisoners knelt amidships—French and Creole sailors, a few too young, a few too proud to beg. Hands bound, faces streaked with salt and smoke.

The men of *The Wraith* stood around them in a ring. No one spoke. Only the creak of hemp and the soft hiss of water against wood.

Redd paced before them like an actor between scenes. His pistol dangled loose, a bit of gold glinting at the hilt. Rain threaded his hair and ran down the line of his jaw.

"Mercy," he said, letting the word hang. "The Devil's share. And the Devil always collects."

A few men laughed—the kind meant to keep the air moving. Elias didn't. He stood near the mainmast, coat dark with rain, eyes following Redd's slow walk.

Redd stopped. "Mr. Grey." The voice carried clean through the weather. "You questioned me once." He smiled without warmth. "Now prove where you stand."

He held the pistol out. Elias didn't move. The weapon found his hand anyway—Redd pressing it into his palm, cold, oiled, already cocked.

"Shoot him," Redd said, nodding toward the line of prisoners. "The boy."

The one he meant couldn't have been more than sixteen. Thin wrists bound with tarred cord, shirt soaked through, hair plastered to his brow. He met Elias's eyes—afraid, yes, but proud enough to hold the look.

"Show them their consequence," Redd said, tone softening to something close to kind. "Every man aboard's watching, Grey. Prove your loyalty."

The deck went quiet. Rain filled the space words had left. Nico shifted near the hatch, a hand resting lightly on the hilt of his knife.

Elias lifted the pistol—slowly, deliberately—and pointed it upward. Rain ticked against the barrel.

"He's yielded," Elias said.

Redd's voice sharpened. "Then finish it."

"He's unarmed."

"Then he won't fight back."

Elias eased the hammer down. The click sounded louder than thunder. "He's under my word now."

The moment stretched, taut and fragile. The rain ran through the scuppers—pink at first, then clear.

"Do it," Redd hissed. "Or die beside him."

Elias met his eyes. "Then you'll prove my point."

The words landed heavy, without bravado. For a heartbeat, no one moved. Then the shift began—small, instinctive. Men slid their feet, found positions that made sense to their hands.

On one side, a knot of Redd's loyalists—too much rum, too little doubt—rested palms on pistol butts, eyes sharp and mean. On the other, Nico stood steady, with Voss hovering uncertain between them. No order was given, but the deck had chosen its lines.

Redd saw it, jaw tightening. Rain streamed off his face as he laughed once, sharp as a bark. "So that's how it is."

He moved before anyone could speak—hand flashing, striking Elias across the face. The pistol fell, hit the planks, and skidded to the scupper with a hollow clang.

"Pick it up," Redd said.

Elias didn't move. "No."

"Mutiny!" Redd roared, and half the guns on deck came up at once. Steel gleamed in the rain.

The ring fractured completely—Redd's men with pistols leveled; Elias's few standing square, water running from hats and sleeves.

"No one fires," Elias said, voice calm but cutting through the rain. "Not for this."

Redd smiled, a small empty thing. "Still preaching."

"I still have my honor."

The rain came harder, flattening smoke from the gunports, turning every face to shadow.

Redd exhaled—something feral behind the breath. "Fine," he said softly. "I'll do it myself."

He bent, snatched up the fallen pistol, and swung it toward the kneeling boy.

Elias lunged, hand outstretched—but too late.

The pistol fired, the flash a brief sun in the gray. The boy snapped backward, chest torn open, breath leaving in a wet gasp. He crumpled sideways, a smear of red in the rain.

Silence—one heartbeat long. Then the world broke.

Nico's pistol barked once, the report swallowed by thunder. A man near Redd staggered, hit the rail, and went overboard. Redd's loyalists fired without thought, shots echoing off rigging and hull.

The deck became smoke and shouting—rain mixing with powder and panic. Men ducked behind barrels, slipped on blood-slick planks. French prisoners screamed—some diving for cover, others frozen in place.

Elias dropped beside the boy, hands already slick, blood hot against his palms. "Hold fire!" he shouted, voice raw. "Cease fire, damn you!"

Nico fired again, covering two wounded men crawling for the rail.

Redd's voice cut through everything—mad, high, unmistakable. "Mutiny! Grey's turned them all!"

He fired into the haze, muzzle flash bright in the downpour.

Rain hissed against hot iron. A barrel near the main hatch spilled its powder, a dark line snaking toward the scupper. Fire licked where it shouldn't have.

Elias looked up, eyes wide. "Nico—!"

But the roar of gunfire drowned the warning.

The ship had chosen her consequence.

CHAPTER ELEVEN

The Burning Sea

T he first flame looked small—a bead of light darting along a wet seam, hissing under rain. Then it found powder dust and tar and stopped pretending to be small.

Fire ran. It traced the plank seams like a fuse, licked the coiled lines, bit into pitch. The smell of burning sugar climbed up, thick and sickly, clinging to the tongue.

"Buckets!" Elias shouted. "Stamp it—keep it off the lines!"

Men moved in blind obedience—boots hammering, buckets sloshing, hands batting sparks that bred faster than fingers could kill them. Redd's loyalists fired through the murk, pistols flaring, shots going everywhere men were. Smoke flattened under the wind and turned the deck into a guessing game.

A rope above them flared like a vein under skin. Fire sprinted up the shrouds, vanished into rain, reappeared higher. *The Wraith's* mainsail took the flame along its leech—an orange wound blooming through gray weather.

"Cut her loose!" Elias coughed, pointing at the lines binding hull to hull.

Two men lunged with axes, then recoiled, hair singeing, heat driving them back like hands.

The first cannonball cooked off by the galley—a muffled thump, heat and fury in one breath. The deck jumped underfoot; a crate of sugar split wide, syrup spilling black and burning, spreading its own slow fire.

"Get the wounded clear!" Elias dragged a man by his collar to the rail and shoved him into other hands.

"Nico—water line—there!"

"I've got it!" Nico's voice cut through, rough and sure.

He and three others worked a barrel to the combing, throwing brine in a steady rhythm. Buckets turned black before they landed. Steam lifted and stuck to skin.

Elias shouldered into the smoke, climbed toward the quarterdeck ladder through falling lines that writhed like struck serpents. Rain hissed; tar popped. A shape stood against the living glow above—coat scorched, face streaked in soot, grin wrong in the throat.

Redd.

"Grey!" he bellowed, voice too big for the ruined air. "You've damned us all!"

He fired into nothing. The muzzle flash lit his eyes, and the ball smashed a useless notch from the rail. He reloaded with a shaking joy that had forgotten why joy exists.

"Leave it!" Elias shouted, hauling himself up the last rungs. "The ship's finished—get clear!"

"You'll die with her," Redd said, smiling like a man who'd won an argument no one else had heard.

Elias seized his collar and wrenched him from the rail. The fabric tore; the man didn't. "You'll take them all with you if you stay!"

Redd twisted free, stumbling toward the shattered hatch, hair singed, eyes fever-bright. "You think you can wear Locke's ghost and call it mercy?" He lifted the pistol again, the gesture almost tender. "Then burn with it."

The shot went wide. The flash did not.

Light kissed the powder trail spilled by panicked hands along the companionway lip. Fire answered with gratitude. It ran—neat as a line drawn by a steady wrist—and dropped below.

The deck inhaled.

A thunderclap of white and orange lifted the quarterdeck and slammed it back. Heat hit like a wall. Elias felt himself thrown, the world turning to brightness and splinters. Ears rang open and empty. Rain became steam and then rain again.

For a single blink, Redd hung in the heart of the blast—arms flung wide against the pillar of fire, face lit the color of iron at forge—then the flame erased him.

The mast shattered. Hoops flew. Rigging fell in burning ropes. The rain came harder, hissing over brightness, making no bargain.

Elias hit planks that had been somewhere else a heartbeat before. The wood burned under his palms; he rolled, gagging, vision spattered orange.

Around him, men crawled—or didn't. The air tasted of salt and iron and sugar turned to poison.

He looked toward the quarterdeck and saw only brightness where a man had been. The ship gave a long, low groan—the sound a great thing makes when it admits the end.

Elias pressed a hand to his ringing ear and forced himself to his knees. Somewhere through the roar, a voice shouted his name; somewhere below, the fire found more to love. Rain stitched needles across his face.

He turned from the light and staggered forward into the smoke.

Balance or burn, Locke had said. The fire had chosen.

CHAPTER TWELVE

The Last Light

The world was red and gold and roaring. Fire climbed the rigging like ivy in a dream, cinders falling in bright skeins that vanished to steam before they touched skin. Deck planks buckled and sighed; seams hissed; the air tasted of tar and salt and iron cooked sweet by burning sugar. The sea around the ship reflected it all—an orange mirror rippling with every breath.

Elias forced himself upright. His ears rang; the blast had left sound a far-off thing, like thunder on another island. Heat pressed close as a crowd. He wiped soot from his mouth with the back of his hand and found the serpent-and-anchor ring beneath the grime, the silver winking once in the glow like an eye opening.

"Nico!" he shouted—or thought he did. His voice felt small against the fire, but it cut through. "Abandon ship! Take the wounded first!"

Nico appeared through the smoke with two men hooked under his arms, faces black, eyes white. He didn't pause to salute or argue. He angled them toward the rail where the davits groaned. "Wounded first!" he threw back, his voice a rope the others could grab.

Hands—burned, shaking, bloody—found lines and blocks. Ropes squealed. The first longboat swung, kissed the scorched hull, swung again. Men lowered in jerks and prayers, boots thumping wood, breath ragged. Another boat began its slow drop beside it, sailors bracing against the davit as if their weight alone could keep steel from melting.

Elias moved where he was needed—steadying a line here, lifting a body there—a shoulder taken without question. That was command now: not barked orders, but hands under weight.

A young sailor froze at the gunwale, eyes gone blank at the space between deck and boat. Elias took him by the shoulder. "Go," he said, calm as he could make it. "That's an order." The boy went.

The hull groaned deeper, the sound running up through the ship's bones into the men's. The tilt grew—starboard sagging toward the sea—sending channels of burning syrup toward the scuppers in black, slow rivers. Rain fell and turned to steam on contact, stitching the air with needles you could breathe.

"Lines clear!" someone shouted from below.

"Room for three!"

"Two wounded—then the rest!" Nico's voice answered.

Elias turned toward the quarterdeck. The blast had gutted it—planks curled like bark peeled wrong, a hole yawning where air burned brighter than day. He thought of Redd, then of work, and chose the work.

He bent to lift a man whose shirt had burned to his skin. The sailor's breath hitched and rattled; his eyes focused for a moment on Elias and found purchase there. "Easy," Elias said. "You're going over." He eased him to the rail, lowered him into waiting arms, felt his fingers let go and forced them to unclench.

A shape moved in the glow. For a heartbeat Elias took it for a tricksome shadow thrown by falling rigging. Then it stepped forward.

Redd.

What remained of his coat clung in scorched strips; hair was singed to wire; half his face wore a mask of soot where sweat had cut runnels. His eyes were the same—bright as flint sparks, unbroken by sense.

"Traitor," he said. The word came out cracked and large. "Traitor!"

Elias turned to face him. "Stay down, Redd. It's over."

"You damned her," Redd rasped, lurching toward him. "You damned me."

"You damned yourself." Elias's voice had no heat to spare. "Mercy has a cost. You set the price."

"Mercy." Redd spat the syllable, as if it burned more than tar. "Mercy is cowardice."

"Maybe," Elias said—and it surprised him that the answer felt like truth. "But it's mine."

Redd's hand twitched. He lifted what had been a pistol—blackened, warped, a piece of iron remembering its former life. The hammer was a ruin. It didn't matter; the gesture was the weapon. "Then pay for it," he said.

Elias stepped forward, not back. Heat wavered between them. He could smell the man's coat—wet wool and char—beneath the stronger kiss of pitch. "If that's the price," he said, "I'll pay it."

The deck cracked open between them. A seam split with a wet sound and orange light poured up, licking at air starved for it. The ship's heartwood showed for an instant—glowing, beautiful, terrible—then shuddered as something deep within gave way.

"Nico!" Elias called without looking. "Stand by!"

He seized the painter line—the last rope holding the nearest boat to the burning hull. Tar had softened it; the fibers were hot under his palm. He pulled his knife with his other hand. The silver ring flashed once—a dull sun through soot.

"Go!" he shouted down into the glow, into the faces tilted up toward him. "Row her clear!"

"Not without you!" Nico's answer came swift, fierce.

"Now!" Elias cut the word like rope.

Redd lunged—a staggering motion, more stubbornness than speed. Elias brought the knife down and severed the painter in one clean stroke. The line snapped back; the boat drifted free, suddenly light without the ship's pull. Nico's head turned once toward Elias, then he set his shoulders and pulled, shouting men to oars.

The hull cracked again, a new seam unzipping with a ripping groan. The deck pitched. Redd stumbled sideways, found purchase on a piece of rail soft as bread, and screamed without words.

A second explosion flared aft—white and consuming, a bloom of light too bright to be seen. For a blink Elias saw Redd outlined against it, arms flung wide as if to embrace a congregation that had left him. Then the light erased him.

Heat hit like a hand. Elias went back, striking the rail with both shoulders. His vision went white, then black, then gray ragged with sparks. Ash landed on his face and melted into the wet there. His breath came in thin, whistled strips. The serpent-and-anchor ring pressed hot into his skin and then cooled.

Sound returned in pieces: the roar of fire, the slap of water, a voice far off counting strokes, another crying a name and letting it be taken.

He rolled to one knee. The deck beneath him had become a map of failure—buckled, charred, impossible. Fire had holes in it now where rain found courage. Cinders floated like ruined snow. The sea beyond was suddenly, eerily calm—a black plate mirroring orange edges.

Below, the boats were pulling clear. He could make out Nico's shape—small, stubborn—bending to the oar, shouting breath into the exhausted. Another boat bobbed in their wake, men reaching over its side to haul a limp shape aboard.

Elias set his back to the rail and watched *The Wraith* burn down to the line where a ship stops and a story starts. The rigging rained cinders. Somewhere deep inside, a last pocket of powder coughed and went out with a sound like a dying laugh.

He raised his hand, wiped soot from the ring, and the silver gleamed a moment—quick, faint—as if remembering another fire a long way from here. "Mercy earns consequence," he said, and the words came quiet—half prayer, half truth.

He took two steps back, steadying himself against the slanting deck. Smoke tore across the wind, curling past him like a curtain drawing closed. The sea below looked black, endless—and somehow merciful.

He dove.

For an instant he was all motion and silence, body cutting through air bright with falling cinders. Then the sea took him—cold, clean, absolute—extinguishing everything but breath and will.

The fire's glow rippled above him as he sank, breaking apart into shards of light that drifted like ghosts through the dark water.

And then there was only the sea, and the sound of it closing.

CHAPTER THIRTEEN

Ashfall

He broke the surface into a world without color.

The first breath came ragged, half water, half air. Salt burned his throat; smoke stung his eyes. The sea was cold enough to hurt—shock running through every limb, turning heat to ache. He kicked once, twice, clearing wreckage—broken spars, burning slivers of rope that hissed as they touched the water.

A wave rolled over him, heavy with ash. He surfaced again, gasping, wiping black foam from his face. The fire behind him turned the sea to copper; its reflection danced on his skin.

Voices carried faintly through the smoke—shouting, then an oar striking hull. He turned toward the sound.

"Grey!" someone called. Nico's voice—hoarse, but alive.

Elias raised one arm. "Here!" The word rasped, swallowed by wind.

Shapes moved through the haze—one of the longboats, half-lit by flame. Two silhouettes leaned over the gunwale, hands reaching. The boat slid close, oars clattering against drifting wreckage.

"Get him!" Nico barked.

A hand caught Elias under the shoulder, another at his collar. Water poured from him as they hauled him in, dead weight turning to breath and coughing. The sea left him shivering on the planks, lungs burning, mind still full of light.

He lay there a moment, coughing out seawater, until the sound of oars found him again—slow, human, steady.

When he lifted his head, the horizon was gray. Smoke drifted like torn cloth. Ash fell in flakes, settling on the black skin of the sea.

He pushed himself upright, hands raw on the boards. The longboat rocked under him, half men, half ghosts. Nico crouched at the bow, soaked and breathing hard.

Elias met his eyes. No words passed between them. He simply reached for the oars.

The blades dipped once, whispering against the water, and the boat moved.

Wreckage drifted all around—charred planks, a half-seared coil of line, the broken jaw of a pinrail. A nameboard bobbed once, blackened beyond reading, then slid under. Far off, something that had been a mast lay like a fallen tree, rigging drooping in burned ribbons. The water made soft, embarrassed sounds as it nudged each piece aside.

Ash settled on his shoulders and clung to the soot there, turning him a winter color. He felt it gather in the hollow of his collarbone, ticklish and cold. He rowed through it, and the wake he carved closed quickly, as if the sea were ashamed of being marked at all.

The serpent-and-anchor ring was a dull black-silver smudge. He turned it with his thumb, and the metal gave back a faint gleam—no more than a blink, an old ember remembering heat.

A shape moved through the haze to port, low and steady: another longboat, stroke matched to breath. Three men pulled at the oars—bandaged, burned, silent. When the boats drew even, their hulls bumped with a sound like a hand on a coffin lid.

Elias kept the oars level and counted without moving his lips. One, two, three—four more behind, hunched and swallowing in little jerks. Faces he knew and faces that had never had time to become anything more than names.

"That's all of us?" he asked. The words felt heavy, like they needed help crossing the air.

Nico shook his head once. "All that's left."

The men didn't look at one another. They didn't look back, either. There was no need; the smoke was doing the only thing it could.

A soft crackle carried over the water—the sound of wet, burned wood cooling. It came from everywhere and nowhere, a thousand quiet endings. No gulls circled; even scavengers knew when a meal wasn't meant for them.

Elias adjusted his grip and pulled again. The oars dipped and rose. A rhythm found him and stayed.

Something knocked the hull and turned in their wake—a barrel, charred on one side, pale where fire hadn't found it. He watched it go and felt nothing he had a name for. Perhaps that was mercy—feeling later, when it can't drown you.

Nico shifted on the thwart, the movement small but loud in the stillness. "Captain," he said.

The word hung there, fragile as ash on air. No one corrected him. No one needed to. The sea, the fire, the choice—they'd done the naming for him.

Elias looked up, and for the first time the title didn't feel borrowed. It fit, heavy but right, like a coat that had been waiting for him all along.

Nico's voice was quieter. "What do we do?"

Ash crossed the space between the boats like a veil. For a moment the younger man's face was mottled white and gray, the ash making a map of scars and soot. The men behind him had turned their eyes to their hands. One thumbed a blister that had burst and left skin like wet paper.

Elias didn't answer until the next pull, then the next. The silence asked better than words. He glanced to starboard where the water darkened—the place *The Wraith* had gone down, the sea there almost black enough to be solid.

"We live with it," he said.

Nico exhaled like a man who'd been trying not to breathe. He nodded. He didn't say thank you; it wasn't that sort of answer. He faced forward, and the oars dipped again, and the boats moved.

A boy lifted his head in the second boat. He couldn't have been more than sixteen—thin wrists, hair pasted with salt and ash, eyes too large for the face around them. A torn coat sat on his shoulders like a blessing that didn't quite fit. One of the captured Frenchmen—alive because Elias had said no when yes would have been easier. His lips moved.

French, just above a whisper. The prayer stumbled like a man in surf, but it kept going. The men around him heard and pretended they didn't. Not from cruelty; because sometimes the only way to hold your own belief is to allow another man his.

Elias reached across the gap with the water skin. The boy hesitated, then took it in both hands and drank as if he didn't trust it to stay full. When he handed it back, he didn't speak. His eyes were bright. He didn't wipe his mouth. The ash did it for him.

"Rest," Elias said.

The boy nodded. He drew the coat tighter—not against cold, but for the memory of shelter—and the prayer found its way back to his mouth and stayed there, quieter now, like a lullaby with no child left for it.

The crackle of cooling timbers faded to an intermittent tic, the ocean's small metronome. Somewhere a plank rubbed another plank and squealed in a thin, complaining voice. The boats rode a long, low swell that didn't care what had burned.

Elias wiped his ring clean of soot with his sleeve. The metal winked once—faint light, warm in a way that had nothing to do with the sun. He remembered the weight of another fire in another story, a blaze that had nothing to do with ships and everything to do with choices. The ring had survived that one, too. Brass remembers.

Nico watched him with the sort of attention that doesn't need eyes. "She's gone," he said. It wasn't a question.

"She is," Elias answered. He didn't say we did what we had to. He didn't say I would do it again. Truth doesn't like being coaxed; it prefers the company of silence.

The two boats fell into a shared rhythm—four oars dipping on one side, four on the other—water parting and returning with the patience of a thing that outlives men. No one kept time. They didn't need to. Tired bodies count themselves.

The dawn couldn't find the courage to turn gold. It stayed the color of breath on a cold morning. Sea and sky blurred so completely that for a few strokes Elias felt he might be rowing into the underside of heaven. Ash continued to fall, finer now, like flour sifted into a bowl that would never be mixed.

Elias glanced back once. A thread of smoke still rose from the place where their world had burned, thin and unwilling to let go. It drew itself upward until the wind took it apart. He watched until it became the same gray as the sky, and then watched a little longer, out of habit.

"Water," he said softly.

Nico passed the skin back across the gap. Hands took it and took it again, each man careful not to drink too much out of respect for the next. The boy took his turn last. He didn't look at Elias this time. Trust had changed the set of his shoulders.

They rowed on.

A gull dared the air and changed its mind. It turned once over the black patch and went inland—white wings cutting a clean line that felt rude in this place.

In the bottom of Elias's boat, ash had gathered around the ribs in delicate drifts. He brushed his fingers through it and they came up gray. He thought of Locke—salt in his beard, the way the old man laughed when a thing he believed proved itself in the world. *Mercy's a choice, lad. Choose it, and the sea will judge the rest.* Elias had chosen. The sea had judged. It was not cruel. It was not kind. It was the sea.

"Captain," Nico said, without looking from his oar. "When we make land—" The rest of it was too heavy to haul over the gunwale. Nassau would have to invent a new word for the welcome that waits for men who set fire to their own luck.

"We'll see," Elias said. "One tide at a time."

Nico nodded, and that was enough. His hands were raw and open in two places. He rowed as if the pain had forgotten him.

The prayer faded to a whisper you could mistake for surf. The men's breathing settled into a pattern that belonged to work instead of fear. The ash didn't stop, but it grew shy of settling on faces; it preferred shoulders, knees, the backs of hands—places that wouldn't argue.

A length of line floated ahead, its fibers swollen with water. Elias feathered the oars and steered around it without a word. No one needed reminding what rope can be made to do.

"Hold this," he said after a time, and Nico's boat matched pace, their hulls touching again, wood to wood. Elias leaned, and the water skin crossed back once more. The boy had fallen asleep sitting upright, fingers worrying a prayer into the torn hem of his coat. One of the men had nudged his shoulder to keep him from tipping overboard without making a ceremony of it.

Elias turned his head toward the place where *The Wraith* had gone under. The sea there had resumed its ordinary business. Even the blackness had loosened to a darker gray. A splinter bobbed up, thought about it, and sank. He watched that, too.

"Mercy earns consequence," he said.

No one answered. The words went out over the water and thinned until they were only air. The oars took up the silence, and the boats moved through it as if through a room in a house they'd lived in all their lives.

The horizon offered nothing but distance. For now, that was enough.

CHAPTER FOURTEEN

The Price of Defiance

They had rowed through the dark for hours—oars whispering through black water that smelled of smoke and rain. The horizon never seemed to move; only the stars shifted, one by one giving way to the first gray of dawn. By the time Nassau's outline rose ahead, the men rowed by habit more than strength, the blades dipping and lifting because hands remembered how.

Dawn spread thin gold across the harbor as the two longboats limped into the shallows, hulls streaked with soot, oars sluggish in the tide. The fort on the bluff stood half-ruined, cannon mouths red with rust. Fishermen paused mid-net haul to stare; whispers passed from skiff to quay. Elias and Nico waded through the surf and pulled the boats onto the littered strand—driftwood, broken shells, tar lumps shining like ugly treasure. The survivors followed, legs unsteady after the night's labor, smoke still clinging to their hair and clothes.

"Home," one of them muttered. The word landed dull and strange, like a coin dropped in mud.

Elias looked up toward the town—the same roofs, the same bell tower—yet the air felt colder for being unchanged.

By midmorning the harbor had chosen its story. Redd's men had reached port first, and lies sprouted like mangrove—quick, many-rooted. *Mutiny. French witnesses. Captain shot.* A merchant glanced at Elias and spat near his boots. Shutters slammed as the survivors passed. Two captains stood on the bluff above the quay and watched with flat faces; when Elias met their gaze, both men turned and spat into the sand.

He tried the market anyway—salt beef, biscuit, clean water, simple things. Prices doubled in a breath. One woman lifting a barrel staved off his coin with a shake of her head. "Not to a traitor, sir." The *sir* was a courtesy that felt like a slap.

A man from the chandlery—someone Elias had bought lines from a month ago—looked at the burns on Nico's hands, grimaced, and closed his door. "Business is business," he said through the plank.

Elias stood in the lane a moment, ash lifting from his coat in the morning heat, and let the door be a wall. Then he turned back toward the strand.

The men scattered along the quay, quiet. Even those who usually reached for laughter as a kind of rope kept their mouths shut.

"We fought for balance," a sailor said to no one in particular. "Seems balance don't pay."

No one answered. No one contradicted him.

The harbor office smelled of ink, damp paper, and old rope. A clerk behind the rail didn't look up at first; when he did, his eyes flicked to the ring on Elias's hand and away again, as if the silver could burn.

"I'm here to address the council," Elias said evenly. "Tell them Elias Grey requests audience."

"The council's adjourned," the clerk replied, shuffling papers that didn't need shuffling.

"Then reopen it."

"They've heard... testimony." The clerk's mouth worked around the word like it was too large. "From Captain Redd's men. From a Frenchman. You're marked mutineer, sir."

"*Sir,*" Elias repeated, half-amused, as if the word had come out wearing the wrong coat.

"I'm sorry," the clerk added—and somehow made the apology worse by saying it softly. "There's nothing here for you."

Behind Elias, near the door, voices hummed.

"That him?"

"Grey."

"Shot the boy with a prayer still in his mouth, they say."

"No—other way."

"Don't matter. Council's done."

The door closed gently on his back as he stepped out, the final form of dismissal.

By afternoon the survivors lingered along the docks like a crew waiting for orders that wouldn't come. A few sold their cutlasses for rum. Others vanished into the alleys with the look of men who wanted walls more than sky. The French boy—wrapped in a borrowed coat, eyes too old—sat on a barrel at the edge of shade. Elias gave him the last of their bread. The boy nodded without speaking and ate slowly, as if bread had rules.

Nico tried to hold a line that wanted to fray. He found six coppers for salve, split them among three men, and secured a bucket of water from a sailor he'd once hauled a line for. Little mercies, small as coins, but they added weight to the day. It wasn't enough.

A man paused beside Elias, swaying. "We did right," he said, then stumbled toward the smell of rum. Another looked at the sea and kept walking until his boots were wet, then turned left and was gone.

Elias let them go. He didn't have a net that could hold grief without tearing.

He checked the boats—thwarts cracked, seams weeping—and touched each gunwale with two fingers, a habit from better days. He spoke low with Nico about where to sleep, how to stretch what little they had. The words felt like nails tapped into soft wood: they held for now; they wouldn't hold long.

Dusk painted the harbor violet and gold. Gulls stooped and argued over an eel head at the tideline, their cries small and far. Heat bled from the sand. The bell above the harbor tolled once and let the sound wander.

Elias stood at the end of the pier, coat open, salt stiffening the hem. The tide worried the pilings with small, patient bites. He turned the serpent-and-anchor ring with his thumb—habit more than thought. Silver caught the day's last light and gave it back as if the metal remembered how.

Footsteps came soft along the planks. Nico stopped beside him, carrying a canvas satchel that had once held powder and now held half their remaining food. He set it down carefully, as if the wood beneath it could bruise.

"They're gone," Nico said. "The ones who stayed sober enough to walk."

"Good," Elias answered without turning. "No one to bury."

They stood together, not touching, watching the harbor do what harbors do: take in, give out, forget the names of ships that leave.

"We did right," Nico said at last. His voice wasn't a question—it was a man setting a thing on the pier between them to see if it would sit level.

Elias's reply came slow, tired. "Right doesn't keep a man fed."

Nico nodded once—acceptance, not agreement.

A breeze moved through the tar smell and carried a taste of rain. Somewhere in town a shutter banged; someone laughed and then didn't. The last light went thin as wire across the water and snapped.

They stayed until the pier was only a darker shape in the dark. Then Nico picked up the satchel, and Elias turned the ring once more, and together they walked back toward whatever shelter the night would lend men like them.

CHAPTER FIFTEEN

The Tavern of Ghosts

R ain came hard and sudden, drumming on the roofs of Nassau and running down the stone gullies like poured glass. The streets smelled of wet limestone and tar. Elias and Nico moved through them with coats drawn tight, boots slapping through puddles that had already gone brackish with sand. Lanterns winked out one by one as they passed—Nassau turning its face away.

By the time they reached the bluff, the rain had gone sideways, carried on a wind sharp enough to sting. At the end of a narrow lane crouched a tavern half-swallowed by rock—its beams warped, its sign faded to ghosts of letters. One shutter hung open and banged in rhythm with the surf. Inside, firelight wavered and a single fiddle note died in the smoke.

Nico hesitated at the door. "We've coin for one night."

Elias pushed it open anyway. "Then we'll make it count."

The sign above the lintel, half-lost to time, read *The Sea's Ghost*.

The warmth hit like a blow. The air smelled of rum, wet wood, and old rope. A handful of locals hunched over cards; a drunk snored with his head on his arms. Behind the bar, a woman in her forties wiped down a counter scarred from a hundred years of arguments. Her hair was a red gone to copper-gray, tied back with a strip of sailcloth. One sleeve was rolled to reveal a rope burn long since healed.

"If you're running from the weather," she said without looking up, "you'll find no mercy in it."

"Not asking for mercy," Elias said, wringing water from his gloves.

The sound of his voice drew her eyes. She looked him over—burned coat, sea-salt still in his beard—and then her gaze caught the serpent-and-anchor ring. Her expression changed, quieting.

"Well," she said slowly. "Haven't seen that mark since the old bastard himself."

Elias froze halfway to the stool. "You knew Locke."

"Knew him," she said, pouring a measure of rum. "Sailed with him. Owed him three debts, paid two." She slid the glass toward him. "Maeve Connolly."

Nico straightened beside him, dripping onto the floorboards. Maeve's eyes flicked to him, assessing, then softened by a degree. "Sit. You look like ghosts come ashore."

They took the corner near the hearth. Steam rose from their coats. The fire's light painted the floor with long stripes, the kind that move when a ship rolls. Elias stared into it until the edges of the room began to fade. When he finally spoke, it came slow, like a man climbing stairs.

He told it plain: the convoy, Redd's madness, the pistol, the flames. No ornament, no plea. Just a list of truths, one after another, each heavier than the last. When his voice faltered, Nico filled the space between sentences.

"He cut the painter line," he said quietly. "Saved what was left of us."

Maeve listened without interruption, elbows on her knees, a clay pipe cooling between her fingers. The bowl still smoked faintly, the scent of rough tobacco drifting through the lamplight. When he finished, the only sound was rain against the windows and the low hiss of the hearth.

She leaned back and took a breath that might have been a sigh. "Locke used to say mercy's the hardest courage. You've got it. But you'll bleed for it yet."

Elias turned the glass in his hand. "Already have."

"Not near enough," she said softly. "Courage doesn't keep a man fed either—but it keeps him human."

For the first time that night, he smiled—faint and tired. "Then maybe there's hope for the both of us."

Maeve snorted and tapped the ashes from her pipe against the hearth-stone. "Hope's a fickle currency. Rum trades better."

She stood and moved behind the bar, rummaging through a drawer of old things—tarnished coins, a bent knife, bits of glass that once belonged to bottles. When she came back, something small rested in her palm.

A wooden disk, no bigger than a biscuit, darkened by age and thumb-worn smooth. A serpent curled around an anchor carved at its center—rough work, but deliberate. The edges were notched where years of handling had rounded them.

"Locke called it ballast," Maeve said, holding it up to the firelight. "Said a man should carry enough weight to keep from drifting."

She turned it once in her hand, then set it gently in Elias's palm. "He carved this the night before Cartagena. Told me balance isn't found in charts or compasses—it's what you hold steady when the storm wants to take it from you."

Elias studied the carving, tracing the serpent's curve with a soot-stained thumb. "He always said the sea remembers the hands that shape it."

Maeve nodded. "Aye. And the hands that try to master it get remembered too—usually in ruin."

Elias closed his fist around the token. The weight was small but solid—warmer than metal, older than coin. "He found the right hands for it, then."

"For now," she said. "See that it doesn't lighten."

Thunder rolled over the bluff, making the beams tremble. Maeve poured another round and set the bottle on the table. "Rest while the world lets you," she said.

Nico sat nearby, eyes fixed on the fire. In the lamplight he saw it—the same steadiness Locke once carried, now living in her. The same certainty that the sea could take everything but the part of you that refused to hate.

Elias turned the token over once more, the serpent-and-anchor catching the flame. "He said mercy earns consequence," he murmured.

Maeve looked at him, one brow raised. "And consequence earns the man."

Outside, the rain thickened, hammering the shutters. The room seemed smaller, warmer, safer for the sound. Elias drank. The rum burned clean and honest, leaving only warmth behind.

The fire popped; thunder answered.

The night settled heavy and waiting—

the calm before the reckoning.

CHAPTER SIXTEEN

The Tide

The rain found every seam in Nassau and worried it open. It rattled shutters, ran off the bluff in thin waterfalls, and beat the tavern roof until the beams answered in a tired creak. Inside *The Sea's Ghost*, the fire turned the windows to orange mirrors where water crawled like quicksilver.

Maeve topped off their cups without asking. The room had shrunk to the sound of rain and the slow talk of wood trying not to warp. Nico sat forward on his stool, eyes on the door as it shuddered in its frame with each gust.

"That storm's got teeth," Maeve said, watching the flames.

"So did the last one," Elias answered. His voice was even; his eyes were somewhere out beyond the harbor, where storms had different names.

Nico rolled his shoulders, a twitch he couldn't hide. "Feels like it's looking for someone."

"Storms always are," Maeve said. "They prefer a face."

A boot scuffed across the porch—quick and wrong. Maeve's head turned. Another footfall. The latch rattled, and the door blew inward on a fist of wind.

A young courier stumbled in, soaked through, hair stuck in ropes to his forehead. He clung to the jamb and sucked air like a swimmer who'd miscounted strokes.

"He's alive," he blurted.

The tavern went still. A card player looked up and froze with a king half-raised.

Maeve didn't soften the question. "Who."

"Redd," the boy gasped. "Burned. Half-blind. Down in the portside alleys—swearing he'll hang Grey by dawn. He's... he's gathering men."

The rain filled the pause that followed, hard as thrown gravel.

Elias set his cup down. The glass barely clicked against the wood.

Maeve's jaw set. "He won't rest till he sees you hang."

Nico's hand had already found the worn grip of his cutlass. "Let him try."

Elias didn't raise his voice; he didn't need to. He only lifted a hand, and Nico's knuckles eased off the leather.

"No," Elias said. "We end it clean."

He stood, testing his balance like a sailor feeling a deck he already knew. From his coat he drew his pistol, cracked the pan, checked the flint. Powder dry. Shot seated firm. The motions were precise, almost tender—the liturgy of a man who respects the tools that end lives and prefers not to use them.

He buckled his coat again—the same burned one from *The Wraith*, cuffs blackened, salt turned white along the seams. Thunder rolled over the bluff, deep as a drum buried under the hill.

You can't outrun the tide, Locke had said once, on a different night with a different storm. The words came back the way old injuries do when the weather turns.

Maeve circled the bar and stood square with him, voice low. "Balance, you said. Even now?"

"Especially now," Elias said.

She studied him a long heartbeat and saw both halves of him at once—the boy Locke had steadied, the man the sea had hardened. She nodded. "Then keep it. Even when it costs you."

"It already has," he said, and there was no bitterness in it. Only fact.

Nico rose, shoulders set. The courier hovered, unsure whether to flee or follow. Maeve reached under the bar, brought up a long oiled cloth, and slid it across the counter. Inside lay a powder horn stoppered tight, a spare flint, and a twist of dry tow.

"For clean work," she said.

Elias tucked the horn into his coat and the flint into his waistcoat pocket. "Thank you."

Maeve's mouth tilted—half warning, half farewell. "Bring back what you can't bury."

"If I'm lucky," Elias said, "that won't be much."

He pulled the door. Rain came in sideways, cold and immediate, needling the skin and flattening the smoke from the hearth. Lightning forked above the ruined fort; the crack of thunder reached them a breath later and rattled the glass in the lanterns.

Elias stepped into it, collar up, stride measured and deliberate, as if the street were a gangplank and the night an ocean that had to be crossed without hurry. Nico followed, head down, hand near his hilt but not on it.

Maeve stood in the doorway and watched them take the lane. She tamped her clay pipe with a thumb, drew once, and let the smoke curl around the doorframe until the rain took it away.

"Locke," she said to the empty room, "your boy's walking into the tide."

The wind answered first. Then the shutters shook. Then the rain swallowed the street, and the door swung slowly shut.

CHAPTER SEVENTEEN

The Reckoning

The storm came like a sail torn loose. Rain hammered the masts until they bowed, wind shrieking through the rigging like a thing that wanted in. Waves slapped the pilings hard enough to shake the barrels stacked above them. Lanterns along the quay smeared into long, trembling streaks of gold across the wet boards.

Elias moved through it with six men at his back, their shapes breaking and reforming in the flicker of lightning. Pistols were wrapped in oiled cloth, blades drawn but low. The smell of pitch and salt clung to everything.

Nico limped beside him, face tight against the pain. Elias looked once; the younger man shook his head before a word could rise between them.

"Keep low," Elias said. His voice carried no louder than the rain. "They'll sweep from the alleys."

They reached the shipwright's yard—half-built hulls under scaffolds, cauldrons of tar guttering against the wind, ropes slapping like loose rigging. Every corner dripped. Every shadow moved. Thunder rolled underfoot, heavy and near.

"Here," Elias said. "Set the line."

The men spread through the wreckage, crouched behind casks and timbers. The wind keened through the ship frames, carrying the smell of iron and oil.

Then came the voices. Distant at first, then growing—Redd's men, rough with rum and purpose, sweeping the waterfront.

"Grey's here!" someone bellowed through the rain. "Find him!"

The first musket cracked, a brief sun in the dark. Splinters leapt from a barrel, scattering across Elias's coat. Another shot answered from the shadows.

"Hold," Elias murmured, raising a hand. He moved between them, calm as a tide. "Wait for the flash, not the noise."

Lightning answered him, white and close. He counted its rhythm with the next volley and motioned. Two of his men rose, fired, and dropped again. Their shots struck true—one silhouette fell into the water, another went to its knees.

Rain swallowed the sound. The air smelled of wet powder and salt.

"Here," Elias said quietly, pointing. "Down. Move with the thunder."

They advanced in short bursts, using the storm itself for cover. Each clap masked their feet. Each flash lit their next refuge.

The storm made everything equal—the righteous and the damned both soaked, both blind.

A musket ball snapped through the dark and hit something hollow; the tar cauldron tipped. Black pitch spilled across the boards and found a waiting lantern.

The explosion of light was instant. Fire ran like liquid gold along the seams, rolled through puddles, and rose in twisting plumes.

"Off the ground!" Elias shouted.

They leapt for the scaffold struts as the tar ignited. Heat washed up through the rain, turning the air to glass. For a breath, night became day. Shadows froze like carvings.

The fire chased Redd's men back through their own smoke, silhouettes flailing. Elias seized the chance, using the blaze as signal.

"Left!" he called. "Cross there—keep tight!"

They moved like parts of one thought, following his gestures rather than his words. Gunfire cracked in the glare, bullets hissing off drenched wood. Elias's small band pressed forward between the flames, each step chosen, deliberate.

The yard was chaos: half-built ships burning, ropes snapping, rain hissing down in sheets that turned every surface to a mirror. It was *The Wraith's* deck again—but this time Elias set the pace, commanding the fire instead of fleeing it.

Nico fired once and winced as the recoil jolted his wounded side. He tried to reload, fumbling. Powder slipped through his wet fingers.

"Slow," Elias said, coming beside him. "Don't rush it."

A crack from the dark. Nico jerked back, blood blossoming through his sleeve. He went down hard behind a keel-block, gasping.

Elias was there before the next shot came. He dragged Nico behind cover, pressed a hand to the wound, and felt the pulse under his fingers.

"Hold it," he said. "You're not finished."

Nico's teeth showed in a grimace. "Wasn't planning to be."

Elias tore a strip from his sleeve, bound the shoulder tight, and tied it off with one quick pull. "You'll live."

"Can't promise the same for them," Nico managed.

Elias gave a small, crooked smile that didn't reach his eyes. "Don't try."

Rain drove the smoke flat, spreading the fire into long ribbons that ran between puddles. The flames threw light on the wet planks, on faces slick with rain and fear. The sea beyond roared, black against gold reflection.

Then came the voice.

It rose over the storm—raw, broken, half rage and half laughter.

"Grey!"

Another crack of thunder.

"Grey! Come die honest!"

The sound carried like a curse.

Elias stood slowly, eyes narrowing through the rain. His pistol hung at his side, the hammer cocked, powder dry. He looked once toward his men—four now, crouched in the glare.

"No spectacle," he said quietly. "End it clean."

They nodded, breath misting in the heat.

Elias stepped out from the cover of the ship frames into the full fury of the rain. Lightning forked above the fort, painting his silhouette against the smoke.

He walked forward, measured, deliberate, toward the sound of the man who would not die.

The flames behind him flickered and hissed, turning his shadow long across the boards. The storm swallowed him halfway, but the rhythm of his boots carried through the water—sure and steady—until the thunder took it away.

CHAPTER EIGHTEEN

Balance

The storm had chewed the wharf into ruin. Fire bled down from the shipyard's upper scaffolds, licking across puddles of pitch while rain tried and failed to drown it. Smoke hung low, sweet with tar. Between the stacked spars, a corridor had formed—narrow, slick, and stinking of heat and brine.

Redd stepped out of that firelight like something dredged up from the deep. His coat hung in black rags, hair plastered to a burned scalp. One eye was milky white, the other bright with hate. A knife glinted in his fist, rain running down its length.

"Mercy's the Devil's share," he said, voice cracking but still sharp.

Elias walked in from the opposite end—soaked to the bone, coat scorched, face streaked with rain and ash. His pistol hung forgotten at his hip. He drew his knife instead—long, balanced, plain steel. The point caught the light once.

"Then I'll claim it."

Redd moved first—a half-snarled roar, more rage than word. His boots hammered across the boards, blade flashing high. Elias met him head-on; the first clash was pure shock—metal on metal, hands jarred to bone. Sparks spat between them and died in the rain.

Elias shoved him back, but Redd came again, hacking, slashing, wild. Steel screeched off hull braces, gouged wood, bit air. Elias ducked one blow that would have opened his skull, turned inside the next, and drove his shoulder into Redd's chest. They slammed against a frame post, the impact sending both knives skittering a heartbeat from their hands.

Redd caught Elias by the coat, snarling through broken teeth. "I'll gut you for what's mine!"

Elias's reply was a short, hard sound—a breath, not a word—as he jammed his knee into Redd's thigh and broke the grip. Redd reeled, slashing again, and the knife found Elias's arm this time—hot pain, quick and deep. He grunted, twisted, and the world narrowed to that moment of distance between them and who moved first.

Elias did.

He drove forward, knife low, blade reversed. Their arms tangled—Redd's strength against Elias's speed. The knives flashed close enough to cut breath; each man's blood washed the other's sleeve. Rain made everything slick, turning the fight into grappling more than fencing: grunts, curses, shoves, steel, hands.

Redd got a hand on Elias's throat. Elias slammed his head forward, broke the hold, and raked his knife across Redd's forearm. Skin parted clean; blood mixed with rain. Redd bellowed, swung wild, and Elias caught the strike with his left hand—felt the blade bite his palm—and drove his own knife up under the ribs.

Redd screamed. The sound was short, hoarse, and stopped too soon.

He hit Elias once—a blind swing to the jaw that sent stars across his vision—then hit the deck hard, splashing in the water pooling between the boards. For a heartbeat he didn't fall; he just stood there, shoulders rigid—then folded forward and landed face-down, the rain taking him.

Elias staggered back against a post, breath tearing out of him. He looked down at his arm—cut deep but clean—and then at Redd. The knife still jutted from the man's side, the hilt trembling with the rhythm of his last few breaths.

Redd rolled to his back, teeth showing, blood thin in the rain. His good eye found Elias again.

"Mercy," he croaked, half a plea, half a curse.

Elias knelt beside him, one hand clutching his bleeding arm, the other reaching for the hilt. "No," he said quietly. "Balance."

He pulled the knife free. Redd gasped once—a sound that might have been laughter or breath leaving for good. Elias reached out and closed the good eye with two fingers.

The rain came harder, drowning the firelight to dull embers. Around them, the last of the yard hissed into darkness. Elias stayed kneeling a moment, breathing hard, staring at the knife in his hand, at the blood and water running down his wrist. He could feel the pulse still racing in his throat—the echo of survival rather than victory.

Behind him, men's voices began to rise—Nico's among them. "Captain! Grey!"

He wiped the blade on his coat and stood, legs unsteady but holding. "It's finished," he called back.

They came slowly through the smoke, eyes wary, faces streaked with rain and soot. One man crossed himself; another looked away. The fire hissed itself dead, and the wind carried the last of the heat out to sea.

Elias sheathed his knife. His hands shook once, then steadied. The serpent-and-anchor token in his pocket felt heavier than it should have—pressing against his thigh like a reminder that balance wasn't peace; it was what you earned after violence, if you were lucky enough to live through it.

Nico met his eyes, wet hair plastered to his brow. "You all right?"

Elias nodded, breath finally slowing. "I will be."

They stood a moment longer—the two of them framed by the dying storm—before moving back toward the shipyard and the men still alive in the rain.

The sea hissed against the pilings below, steady and patient.

Above it, the world went quiet again.

CHAPTER NINETEEN

The Weight

Morning rinsed Nassau but did not clean it. Smoke still clung to the harbor, thin as a bruise. Fort Nassau's hall—half-roofed, plank walls furred with salt—smelled of damp powder and old rum. A long table bowed in the middle from years of weather and weight. Captains gathered where they could fit: Jennings with his neat hat and needle gaze; Hornigold heavy at the head, rings cutting little moons in his fingers; three petty kings of Nassau wearing plumes gone to wet ropes; a scatter of mates and hangers-on who had learned to look serious when they smelled blood.

Elias stood in the open space the hall kept for trouble. His coat was scorched, ash ground into the seams; a clean strip of linen circled his forearm where Redd's knife had found him. The serpent-and-anchor ring on his hand held a dull shine in the gray light. Nico stood at his shoulder, pale but upright, sling tight, jaw set for silence.

The murmurs wound down. Hornigold rapped a knuckle on the warped table and liked the sound of it.

"We're told," he said, "there was a mutiny. We're told you killed your captain."

Elias let his breath out slow. "A man who'd already killed his crew," he said. "The rest of us chose to live."

A few faces twitched. One of the petty kings smirked like a man who'd seen a better play.

Jennings leaned his forearms on the table, polite as a knife on a plate. "We'll have witnesses," he said. "If Nassau still pretends to justice."

Doors at the back grumbled. A clerk—ink-stained fingers, tidewater shoes—brought the first.

A dockhand came in, hat in hand, hair slicked to his head by sea-sweat you can't wash out. "Saw him, I did," he said to the table more than to Elias.

"Dragged men off the planks when the pitch went—and not just his." He glanced at Elias as if he'd broken some smaller law. "Didn't have to."

"Names," Hornigold said, bored already.

The dockhand shrugged. "Names burn same as rope."

They sent him off with a grunt.

The next man was thinner, skin the color of oiled hull, chest bound in clean cloth. He moved carefully, as if breaths cost. A rescued Frenchman. His English came in bricks carried one at a time.

"He... stop," the man said, holding a hand up, palm out, for the word itself. "Stop killing. My boy—" The breath hit a seam; he crossed it. "My boy live."

He was led away, eyes low, shoulders unashamed.

Two of Redd's men were marched in last of the first lot—shaken hard by the night, shock making their mouths honest. They had the look of lads who had never been asked to speak in halls and didn't like the way it made their hearts show.

"Grey ordered guns quiet," one said, voice rough. "Could've run us through. Didn't."

"Redd were mad," the other muttered, then swallowed the rest like a fishhook. "Sir," he added—and nobody knew whether the word belonged to Grey, the council, or an idea of law that had lost its boots.

The room tilted. Murmurs changed color. Men who had come to taste blood found themselves chewing something else: the grit of facts. Jennings turned his head a fraction, studying Elias as if measuring a hull by sight.

Hornigold felt the shift and didn't like the angle. His scowl settled in deeper. "The Articles say what they say," he growled. "Captain's word aboard ship—"

"—isn't law when it's murder," a woman's voice cut in, low and hard.

Maeve Connolly stepped out from the side door, coat shoulders beaded with rain, clay pipe stem showing like a bookmark from her pocket. She looked small near the table and larger than any man in the room by force of what she'd kept intact. Eyes moved to her and then away, the way men glance at a gale and pretend it's a breeze.

"You want to talk Articles?" Maeve said, walking closer, boots leaving dark ovals on the warped boards. "Ask yourselves when Nassau last honored any that weren't convenient."

A petty king shifted his plume as if that could hide him. No one answered. The hall listened because it couldn't think what else to do.

Maeve planted a hand on the wet edge of the table. "Balance isn't softness. It's the cost you're willing to carry." She nodded once toward Elias without granting him the grace of looking long. "Locke taught that to men better than us—and Grey remembered when the rest of you forgot."

Eyes found the ring then, the serpent wound round the anchor—old silver in a ruined hall. A few captains looked away like men who'd stumbled on a grave and read their own names.

"The mark meant something once," Maeve said, softer and more dangerous for it. "Might again, if Nassau can stomach what mercy costs."

Silence held. It wasn't comfortable. It had weight. A gull yelled outside and got no answer from the room. Jennings cleared his throat in a gentleman's fashion. "We've heard enough," he said to no one and everyone. "Unless Captain Hornigold prefers more men dragged in to say the same with different mouths."

Hornigold's jaw worked, chewing pride. He glanced down the table and found no help, only captains sitting on their hands to keep from waving with whichever way the wind had turned. The storm had taken the roof; the night had taken Redd; now the room took its cue from anything still standing.

"Nassau's short of ships," he said finally, like a man setting down a weight he meant to lift again. "See you don't waste one."

It was not a verdict. It was less dangerous than forgiveness and more useful than law. Chairs scraped. Plumes shook rain. The council dispersed like gulls after a squall—sudden, hungry for old talk: storm damage, shares, which hulls could be saved before worms found them.

Elias did not move. The sound of boots on the boards faded; the smell of rum rose as if the room itself had exhaled. Nico stood quiet at his side, the sling a white slash against his coat. He looked older than he had the night before—not by years, but by edges.

Maeve came to them last, mouth a straight line that wasn't displeasure, only truth. She tipped her chin toward Elias's wrapped forearm. "You'll need clean thread," she said.

"I have some," he answered.

"Bring your own needle," she said, and left through the side door with a scuff of boot that sounded like approval because she hadn't bothered to make it sound like anything else.

Jennings paused by Elias as he passed and tipped his hat a fraction—no more than a man might give the weather for clearing. "Let the sea decide the rest," he said. Elias nodded. It was the only court any of them respected for more than a week at a time.

The hall emptied to the ghost sounds of old musters—voices that would never be back to make the same mistakes twice.

Nico exhaled. It left him thinner, steadier. "Was that—" He searched for the word and found the one the night had taught him. "Mercy?"

Elias watched the door where Hornigold had gone, then the light across the warped table, thin as a blade and twice as cold. He turned the ring with his thumb, feeling the old grooves where another man's life had worn truth into metal.

"Balance," he said. "Sometimes they look the same."

Nico nodded, slow. He looked out the broken strip of window where the harbor showed its gray face. "What now, Captain?"

There was no swagger in the title; it fit because the sea and blood and fire had cut it to measure. Elias listened. The fort stones ticked as they dried. From below drifted the sounds of men rebuilding what they could.

"We find a hull," Elias said. "Something that'll take a keel straight and forgive what we ask of her."

"Short of ships," Nico echoed, with the ghost of a smile.

"Then we waste nothing," Elias answered, and his voice went quieter without losing strength.

They stepped out into the post-storm light. The air tasted of rain and tar and a morning that didn't care what men called justice—only what they built before dark. Down the hill, the shipyard lay in wet angles and black streaks, a half-burned brig on her side like a sleeping beast dreaming of water. Men moved like ants, carrying order to where the night had left none.

Behind them, the hall remembered the last word spoken in it and held it in the grain a while—the way wood remembers every tide it has resisted. Ahead, the harbor breathed: patient, unafraid, as if to say the sea keeps no grudges but all accounts.

Elias started down toward the yard, Nico keeping his shoulder even with his. The ring was warm on his hand. The cut on his forearm stung honest. Somewhere in his pocket the little wooden disk pressed against his thigh—weight enough to keep a man from drifting.

Balance, not mercy. A ship, not a speech. Work first. Then the tide.

CHAPTER TWENTY

A New Course

Morning rinsed the harbor but left the smell of tar and rain. Steam lifted from the flats. The broken fort on the hill looked less like a tooth and more like a warning. Down in the shipyard, gulls hopped among coils of line and driftwood, stabbing at whatever a night storm leaves behind.

She lay half on her side in the mud, a blackened hull with one crooked mast still clinging to the day. The other had snapped and slid under like a splint. The deck was a burned scab, hatch coamings charred to the color of old coffee. But below the waterline the planking rang true when you rapped it—sound where it mattered.

"A carcass," the yard foreman said. "You'll get splinters and ghosts for your coin."

Elias walked the length of her in the tide's faint lap, hand trailing across ribs still warm where the sun had found them. He noted the curve of the run aft, the straightness of the keel through the slime. He knelt and pressed his palm to a scorched plank; heat came back into his skin like a pulse.

"She floats on a full tide," he said. "That's a beginning."

The foreman laughed the way men laugh when they smell trouble that isn't theirs. "Scrap price, and you clear the slip before next moon. You drift into my neighbor's berth, I send your debt walking on your shoulders."

Elias loosened the string of a small pouch, tipped silver into the man's hand, and offered the promise with his voice. "We'll give her a second life."

"Waste your back if you like," the foreman said, weighing both. "She'll still answer to the sea before she answers to you."

"Then we'll learn her language," Elias answered, and turned toward the water with something like relief.

Days slipped their knots and ran into weeks. The yard found its old rhythm—hammer, saw, tar, tide. A crew gathered around work the way men gather around heat.

They cribbed her hull with timber blocks as the tide fell, and when it rose again they looped under-belly slings from yardarms rigged to a pair of stubborn pines. Lines creaked, water burped from seams, and the brig grudged on her side another finger's width toward upright. They worked the tide like a jack, lifting a little each day and blocking before the sea could take back what it had given.

Nico moved through it like current—arm bound early, then unbound and stiff, grin returning in fits. He kept tools moving and tempers tied off. "Pump the bilge before you strain the lines," he'd bark, then pass a bucket and pump himself for good measure. "Mind the frames. That brace will bite if you let it."

They ripped off the worst of the deck and laid stringers new and narrow. Elias chalked on planks the lines he wanted: a leaner stern, slightly raised foredeck for green water, frames shaved where weight grew lazy. He drew a rig in charcoal on a tar barrel: twin square tops, a driver aft cut deep and clean, stays smartened for quick hands. A brigantine's bones with a hunter's lungs.

"She'll outrun the law if the wind owes us a favor," Nico said, peering at the sketch.

"She'll outrun fear if we handle her honest," Elias answered, and he meant the ship and the men both.

They scavenged a foremast from a sloop that had washed in near Hog Island—straight island pine with enough spring to forgive a bad gust. They planed it in the shade until white shavings curled around their ankles like surf. Spars came from everywhere—castoffs, trades, a length of yardarm bought off a fisherman who needed rum more than leverage. Blocks were rebuilt with boiled linseed and care; ropes were spliced until the ends remembered they were one.

Tar kettles hissed; the smell climbed the back of the throat and stayed there. Caulkers walked bent-backed with mallets and irons, beating hemp home into seams that drank pitch like thirsty men. The sound—tap-tap-TAP, tap-tap-TAP—ran through the yard from dawn until the bell above the quay gave up and let evening take the work.

Maeve came once a week with the weather in her coat and the tavern on her breath—two bottles under one arm, a roll of sailcloth under the other, advice like small knives. "You're lightening the deck too fast," she said once, hands on her hips. "We're building a hunter, not a brag." Next time: "Shorten that staysail or it'll slap you stupid in a squall." The third week she didn't correct anything; she only stood on the quay, smoked her pipe down to its last stubborn ember, and said, "She's lighter than sin now. Name her careful."

Men peeled off as they always do—one for a woman, one for a grudge, one because the work felt too much like prayer and he'd never liked churches. Enough stayed. The ones who stayed learned to read the tide by the damp lines on the pilings, to lift with their legs and swear with their mouths, to keep a steady heat under tar so it didn't break into flame and argue its case with the whole yard.

Elias worked in his shirt when the sun bullied through cloud, sleeves rolled, forearm scar pink under fresh scab. He carried, he planed, he held ladders and lines, and when men looked up for orders, half the time he was already there, shoulder in the same rope. "True on that line," he'd say, not loud. "She'll thank you in a head sea." Or, "Let the wood choose its own bend; don't force it to lie." His voice stayed even; his hands stayed busy; his ring stayed dark with pitch until the water could find it.

Nights were for sore muscles, lamplight, and a ledger on his knees. Names and marks, wages and shares, notes on timber bought and rope repaired. He wrote with slow care, as if the ink had weight, and when he was done he'd sit and listen to the hull creak as it settled—an animal dreaming of running again.

Rain came and went, polite as a landlord. It found every seam they missed, and the yard smelled clean after. When the sun broke through long enough, they hauled a patched triangle of canvas up a jury stay to dry, and it snapped once like it had remembered applause.

On the twenty-second morning, the tide took her weight clean. The last shore line slacked and fell, and the half-burned brig—new deck laid, seams packed and tight, rig rising in a simple statement—floated on her own keel. She sat light, a touch higher forward than she would when guns and water and food had their say. But she floated true. The men stood and watched her bob with the small wind-chop like a creature sniffing at freedom.

A hat went up and came down in a puddle. Someone barked a tune and lost the air halfway through; no one minded. The foreman who'd sold them the carcass crossed himself, then pretended he had an itch. "She's a ghost," he muttered.

"Then she'll haunt the wicked," Elias said, and didn't smile.

He posted the share list on a tar barrel by the main partner. The ledger lay open and clean beneath it. "Equal shares," he said to the men gathered—twenty-two now, a few with new scars and all of them with old debts. "Written. Witnessed. No king. No flag besides ours."

A handful of eyes cut toward the ruined fort. A few more toward the harbor where Redd had gone under all of them. "Balance," Elias said, and the word carried farther than a shout could have.

They came one by one to touch the ledger and sign or mark—some with names they learned in jail, some with Xs they'd earned at sea. A tall man with a scar that tugged his lip signed Voss with the blunt tip of a shipwright's pencil. A boy no older than the Frenchman's son made an X like a mast and stared at it as if it might grow a sail. Nico pressed his whole palm flat on the page before he remembered himself and laughed. "For luck," he said. Elias left the print where it landed.

"Wages come from shares," Elias said, closing the book. "And shares come from work. We cut old habits off at the wrist and let them bleed out. Anyone wants a tyrant, put on a wig and go find one." He let their grins rise and then fall. "Anyone wants a home, build it with your back."

No cheer followed. The men simply turned to their tasks and made the idea true.

By the fifth week the rig stood like a promise—short masts, stout shrouds, stays snug. The driver's boom sat low and eager; the foretops looked like blades. Gunports framed the deck where guns would go one day when coin and caution found each other, but for now the space stayed open—speed where slaughter had once lived. The stern came in tighter, lines pared, a hint of lift to her run that would make her dance when the wind tried to bully her.

At sunset the yard went gold. Fresh pitch drank light; tar lines shone like wet rope. The men gathered aft with a bottle that had started fuller and a hammer that felt like an oath. The transom was bare, planed smooth, waiting.

Nico stood beside Elias, sling gone, motion back in the arm if not yet strength. He tapped the transom with the hammer, soft. "She's too fine to stay nameless, Captain."

Elias looked forward and aft, down the lane of her deck, across the rig, out to the harbor mouth where a first star blinked through the haze as if testing whether it wanted to be seen. He tasted soot and salt, heard the ropes talk in small voices along the pins, felt the deck give the right amount under his feet.

"She's not what she was," he said. "She's what's left of what we are."

The star above the channel steadied. He saw it reflected broken in the puddles on deck and whole in the narrow water beyond the quay. "*The Specter*," he said.

The men repeated it low, once and again, like surf finding a new pattern along a beach. A shipwright with hands like mallets took a marlinspike and carved the letters in deep cuts, slow. Nico smeared the grooves with tar, and the name went black and gloss-smooth against the new-grained wood. The tide lifted her while they worked, and she leaned into the small weight of the evening breeze as if she'd heard her name and wanted to answer it.

They passed the bottle and let it go empty without ceremony. Someone spat over the side for luck; someone else said a prayer he'd learned from a priest who had died poorly. Maeve stood on the quay with her pipe, watched the letters emerge, and flicked ash like a blessing she'd deny if asked.

Night came on honest. Lanterns struck sparks into the dark. Tools lay stacked in neat heaps that said tomorrow had plans. Ropes lay coiled like sleeping things. Men stretched on the deck where a warm board remembered sun, looking up at the harbor lights as if counting stars that had chosen to roost ashore.

Elias walked the length of her alone. The serpent-and-anchor ring caught lamp glow and made it look like something remembered rather than reflected. In his pocket, the little wooden token Locke had carved pressed a small warmth against his thigh—the sort of ballast a man carries because drop it once and you never find it again.

At the gangway, Nico waited. "She's ready for sea," he said with the grin of a boy who can already taste the spray. "Not far. A trial. Enough to learn her temper."

"Soon," Elias said. He put his hand to the rail and felt it answer, a thin vibration that traveled into the bones of his wrist. "Let her rest on the tide first."

Nico nodded because he understood: ships are animals, and you don't run one the day you teach it to stand.

Below, the harbor made that slow, patient sound it keeps for men who have chosen to stay alive. Beyond the reef, the sea wore a pale line where moonlight thought about being generous. *The Specter* rocked once, breathed, and settled—wood speaking to water in a language older than the men who listened.

"Balance," Elias said under his breath, testing the word against the night.

The ship answered with the quiet creak of living timber.

Work had turned ruin into a hull; time would turn a hull into a ship; the sea would make a captain or refuse him. For now, under a sky that had decided to be clean, a ghost found her shape and learned the tide's name.

In the morning there would be paint and rope ends and argument. Soon after, canvas. After that, horizon.

For the moment, the yard grew still. The hammer's echo faded into the pilings. Lanterns burned down. The tide rose another thumb's width and held.

And *The Specter*, black and lean and breathing, kept her quiet vigil at the edge of open water.

Epilogue

The sea was clean again. Not calm—never that—but honest. Swells rolled slow and deliberate, sunlight sliding over them like oil on steel. The air smelled of salt and pitch and the kind of wind that keeps a man awake.

The Specter—born of ruin, made new by labor—shouldered through it with a hunter's grace. Her patched canvas drew full, seams whispering as they filled. Every board and rope still smelled of tar; every line hummed a new name under strain.

Behind her, Nassau had already begun to shrink—smoke curling thin from cook fires, the broken fort on the hill a chipped tooth in the island's grin. The reef glittered white at its edge, and then even that was gone, lost in the wash.

Elias stood at the helm, coat open to the breeze. The serpent-and-anchor ring caught the first true light of morning and threw it back at the sea. He leaned one hand on the worn rail and felt the wood answer—alive and restless beneath him.

Nico moved nearby, coiling line in neat turns that refused his tune—he was humming off-key, the same tune he'd butchered every time since the yard. The men went about their work with that tentative rhythm common to new crews and new faith: the quiet testing of both.

A shout came from the forecastle. "Flag ready, Captain!"

Elias turned. A strip of dark cloth waited in a sailor's hands—stitched by candlelight back in the yard. He nodded once. "Run her up."

The halyard rattled. The black flag unfurled against the new sun—its design simple, bold: a silver serpent curled around an anchor, the symbol cut clean and deliberate. No crown, no cross, no border. Their own.

Wind caught it, snapped it taut, and for a breath it shimmered like a blade.

"No king," Nico said softly. "No flag besides ours."

Elias smiled faintly. "That'll do."

He reached into his coat and drew out Locke's brass compass. The lid clicked open; the glass was clouded with salt, the needle uncertain. It wavered, stuck once, then found its place and held true. He smiled—small, private. "Mercy earns consequence," he said. It came out less like a warning now, and more like a course to steer by.

Nico looked up from the coils. "Say again, Captain?"

"Nothing that needs repeating."

He set the compass aside and took the wheel, feeling the ship's weight answer—solid, willing. The wind came steady off the beam. *The Specter* leaned into it, her hull hissing through the swell.

The serpent-and-anchor flag streamed high above, bright against the endless blue. Below it, the crew worked in quiet rhythm—men no longer running, only moving forward.

The horizon opened ahead—blue on blue, limitless. The sea judged nothing, forgave nothing, and offered everything.

Elias looked once over his shoulder—the island gone to haze—and then forward again. His ring flashed once in the light.

"Balance," he murmured.

The Specter answered with the creak of living wood.

And with that, she sailed on—a new name on the water, a legend beginning to breathe.

www.ingramcontent.com/pod-product-compliance
Lightning Source LLC
Chambersburg PA
CBHW070644130626
46555CB00006B/2704